Watching my Wife in Jamaica

By Victoria Kasari

ISBN: 1500831476

ISBN-13: 978-1500831479

DEDICATION

With thanks to TB and Walt for their suggestions

ALSO BY VICTORIA KASARI

Cuckolded - My Wife on the Oil Rig
Cuckolded - My Wife at the Renaissance Faire
Cuckolded - Watching My Wife
Cuckolded 2 - My Best Friend's Wife
Cuckolded in College
Cuckolded By My Boss (Four Part Series)

The Cuckolded in Revenge Trilogy
Locked Up and Cuckolded
Feminized and Cuckolded
Sissified and Cuckolded

Blurbs and free extract at the end of this book!
Can't find a story? http://victoriakasari.com

6

CHAPTER 1

"Be honest," said Kim. "Is it okay? Or is it too sexy?"

The answer was both. I loved the way the blue dress clung to the small of her back before skimming over her curving ass. I couldn't take my eyes off the neckline, where her softly tanned skin made her breasts seem even more alluring next to the dark fabric. The neck was only an inch or so above her nipples, and gathered and lifted them to present an alluring display of cleavage.

And that was the problem. The dress was mouth-watering, from the low neckline to the high hem, Kim's smooth, elegant legs visible right up to mid-thigh. It was better than okay. I loved it. But it was too sexy, in her eyes. I could tell from the way she asked the question. If she bought it, she'd never wear it. My wife just wasn't that sort of woman.

"It's maybe...a little too revealing," I said, trying to keep the regret out of my voice.

Kim turned and gave me one of her knockout smiles. "I knew it. Thanks, honey." And she flounced back into the fitting room to try the next one. I slumped down on the boutique's couch, dropped the shopping bags between my feet, and sighed.

I couldn't be angry at her. I was blessed with a gorgeous wife, the sort of woman who turns heads everywhere she goes. If anything, I was mad with myself, for wanting her to dress differently. I mean, aren't us guys meant to be over-protective? Aren't we meant to cover our women up, if anything, to stop some other guy stealing them away? So why, whenever we went to the mall together, did I find myself wishing she'd take a few more risks?

I had a nasty feeling I knew the reason. After ten years of marriage, were things starting to go a little...stale? Predictable? Was this the time I was supposed to start buying whips and handcuffs, in an effort to "spice things up?"

I winced. It sounded cheesy. I didn't want us to be one of *those* couples, desperately trying to find something to re-ignite the fire. The fire had burned just fine by itself when we'd first met. Hell, the sex had been great right up until the last year or so. But I couldn't deny that things had slowed down from a few times a week to a few times a month. Was that why I wanted to see Kim in sexier clothes? Because I was *bored* with her?

I knew that was wrong. I didn't want some other woman. How could I? At 32, Kim looked, if anything, more gorgeous than when I'd first met her. Her honey-blonde hair hung down in soft waves almost to her lower back. Those dark green eyes, the shade of a verdant forest, had lost none of their ability to stop me in my tracks. And that body: flaring hips and an ass you wanted to squeeze with both hands. Full, firm breasts that I couldn't stop looking at, especially when she wore one of her tight sweaters. I didn't want anyone else. I wanted her. I just...wished she'd show herself off a little more.

Show herself off a little more?! Why? So that other men could envy me? I was pretty sure I wasn't *that* insecure. Why, then?

I shook my head again. Recently, it felt like I didn't know *what* I wanted.

Kim emerged from the fitting room again, this time in a dress whose neckline was a good inch higher, its hem falling to the knee. It was a lot less sexy, but it was also exactly the sort of thing she liked.

"What do you think?" she asked happily. "Perfect, right?"

I sighed. "Yeah," I said. "Perfect."

***

We sauntered through the mall, our arms full of shopping bags. When I saw our reflections in one of the plate glass windows, I couldn't help thinking that we looked like the perfect suburban couple...but not perfect in a good way. Perfect in a predictable way. Mr and Mrs. Selman. Kim with her long, blonde hair and hourglass figure. Me, a little taller than her, my dark hair cropped respectably short. We had a nice house, two well-paid jobs—her in finance, me in engineering—a BMW we were still paying off and no kids yet. We ate in the same chain restaurants and watched the same TV shows as about a million other couples. Hell, the marketing men probably had a category especially for us.

Our lives were safe. Predictable. *Boring?* Was that the problem—that we never took any risks? Sometimes I felt like life was just passing us by, that I was going to wake up one day and suddenly be forty, then fifty, then—

I glanced across at my wife. She seemed happy enough, but the lack of sex had to be bothering her, too. Or something else was bothering her and that was causing the lack of sex.

Something had to change.

There are moments when random chance shifts the path of your life forever. As I looked again at our reflection in the window, I saw something reflected behind us. White beaches. Azure sea. Palm trees. It was as if we were there.

I slowly turned around. Directly behind us, a huge screen in the window of a store was running a travel commercial on loop. Happy, smiling couples who looked a lot like us ran through the surf. Waiters passed exotic cocktails into waiting hands.

I look back on that moment now and wonder how our lives would have been different if the commercial had been for Paris, or Vegas, or Mexico. But it wasn't. The friendly, welcoming logo at the end said "Jamaica."

"What if...we took a vacation?" I said slowly.

***

We went into a coffee shop to talk about it. It was June and already hot enough that we ordered iced lattes, even in the air-conditioned mall. The perfect time to take a vacation.

"We need one," I reasoned. "We've both been working too hard."

We had. I figured it might be one reason why things had cooled down in the bedroom. And even if it wasn't, getting out of LA for a while could only help, right?

Kim bit her lip. "It's just so sudden," she said. She sat down on one of the leather couches and her skirt lifted a little way up her legs, showing off smooth, toned thigh. "Weren't we going to save the money, this year? Towards...you know."

We'd talked about maybe starting a family later that year. Kim had already come off the pill, and we'd switched over to condoms in preparation for trying. Recently, though, sex had been so infrequent that the idea was academic.

Kim noticed her skirt, and tugged the hem down. My heart sank along with it.

"It won't cost that much," I said quickly. "Not if we book some last-minute flights." I started tapping on my smartphone screen, looking at prices. "Can you get a week off—from the twenty-fourth?"

Kim's eyes widened. "Next *week?*" she squeaked. "You're talking about going next week?!"

I understood her surprise—being impulsive wasn't like me at all. We were the sort of couple who planned *everything.* But seeing the commercial had gotten me all fired up. I could still see it through the coffee shop window and, as I watched, a woman ran in slow motion across a beach, her breasts jiggling in a barely-there bikini.

Kim narrowed her eyes as she saw me looking. "I know why *you* want to go," she murmured, but there was a teasing smile on her lips.

I flushed a little, but the irony was that she was wrong: I wasn't interested in the model in the ad. I was thinking about how Kim would look, if I could persuade her into something similar. Maybe, in a foreign country, away from it all, she'd be a little more...experimental.

"Call your boss," I said. "Let's do this,"

***

It was the fastest I'd ever booked a vacation. The fastest I'd ever booked *anything.* In the time it

11

took to finish our iced lattes, we had flights and a hotel booked, leaving in less than a week. Then, since we were already in the mall, we started shopping for shorts and t-shirts, sunglasses and sunscreen. Both of us were a little giddy with excitement. That morning, we'd strolled into the mall to pick up a few things. Now we were looking forward to seven days on the beaches and in the bars of Jamaica...a country I knew next to nothing about.

I ordered a travel guide, so that we wouldn't be going in completely cold. But Kim's smile was reassurance enough. As long as it was hot and fun, I didn't really care what else the place did or didn't have. I just wanted us both to relax, let our defenses down and get back to how we used to be, a few years before.

***

It's funny, in hindsight. We did relax. We did let our defenses down. But instead of getting back to how things used to be, Jamaica ensured our relationship would never be the same again.

CHAPTER 2

"You're sure?" I asked, blinking in disbelief. "There's nothing together?"

The check-in attendant shook her head. "Nope. But I'll put you as close together as I can."

That turned out to be four rows distant.

"It's no big deal," said Kim. "It's only four hours until we switch flights in Atlanta. Can you sit us together for the second leg?"

The check-in attendant checked and nodded.

I told myself that Kim was right—what did it matter if we were sitting apart for a little while? It wasn't as if we were a honeymooning couple who needed to hold hands. It was a minor upset in what would be an otherwise perfect vacation.

So why did it feel like such a bad omen?

***

We boarded from the rear, so I got to take my seat first and watch as my wife sat down. We both in row "C": aisle seats, but she was four rows in front of me. An old couple took the two seats next to her. Then *he* walked up.

A Texan, judging by the Stetson. Bigger than me and a lot bigger than Kim, especially because she was already sitting down and he was standing, holding his carry-on bag in one hand as if it didn't weigh a thing. I saw his eyes go to the old couple next to Kim, who were talking amongst themselves. I could almost see the cogs turning in his head. *She's on her own.*

I followed his gaze. Kim was wearing a soft gray vest top with a pink cardigan around her shoulders. It was fairly demure but, from the angle he was staring down from, the scoop neck would give him a great view of the soft, dark valley between her breasts. And though she'd tugged her denim skirt down her thighs as soon as she sat down—as she always did—I could see his eyes sweep down her body to those long, shapely legs. He looked all the way down them...and then back up to the spot where they joined.

"Well now," he said, grinning widely enough to show white teeth. "You mind if I slot this thing in your space, li'l lady?"

Kim blinked and reddened. The guy showed her his carry-on bag, faking innocence, but the thinly-veiled come-on clearly wasn't lost on her. She shrugged wordlessly, glancing up at the overhead locker.

The cowboy pushed his bag into the space, slammed it shut, and then took a seat...right across the aisle from my wife.

I sat there blinking. It was obvious that he was coming on to her...and that he mistakenly thought she was alone on the flight. I knew what I had to do. I had to go over there and make it clear that Kim was my wife. I didn't need to get into a fight over it, just walk up and put my hand on her shoulder or give her a kiss—just enough to let him know he'd made an error. Then he'd leave her alone.

I knew all that in theory. But in practice...something else was going on. In practice, I watched the cowboy staring at my wife, drinking in every inch of her body, even demurely wrapped as it was...and I was turned on. *Really* turned on. I could feel my cock swelling and hardening with each second that I watched them. It was like...the nearest I can get to the feeling is that it was like watching a deer, being stalked by a lion. I had a hold of the deer, on a long, fragile rope, and I could jerk it out of danger...or I could watch things unfold.

The tension of it, of knowing that he wanted to grab her...kiss her...*fuck* her. Knowing that I could stop it at any time, just by getting out of my seat and going over there...and yet wanting, for some reason, to wait, to watch just a few more seconds, then a few more again.... I found I was actually leaning forward in my seat.

The flight was filling up, now, and things were getting noisy. I couldn't hear the cowboy when he spoke, but it looked like a friendly question—*where are you from,* maybe. My wife looked round at him and then, just for an instant, I saw her try to glance back at me. Maybe she wanted to check I wasn't annoyed. But with me directly behind her, it was awkward—she'd have to crane right out of her seat to even see me.

So she gave up. And, to my surprise, I felt relieved.

I didn't want this to end. Not right away.

She looked across the aisle and said something back to the cowboy, a throwaway response designed to shut him down. But it didn't matter. He was far too pushy, far too practiced in seducing women to

15

let a little resistance stop him. What do they call that sort of guy? An alpha male? I actually had a better view of him than I did of her, since he was diagonally across the aisle from me. His muscles pushed out the front of his crisp white shirt—much more tanned than me. Maybe he really did work on a ranch or something. He had his sleeves rolled up to his elbows and his forearms were thick and rugged, especially when he rested one on the armrest of his seat, only a couple of feet from my wife's own slender arm.

I should stand up, I thought. *I should go over there and stop this.*

But then the seatbelt sign came on and I immediately fastened mine, and told myself that now it was too late.

The cowboy made a big show of not being able to figure out how his seatbelt worked. He said something to my wife and I saw her shake her head. Then he said something else, raising his hands in helplessness, and Kim laughed, throwing her head back in a way that made her long, honey-blonde hair catch the light. I saw her stand halfway up, and then she was leaning right across the aisle and into the cowboy's seat, her hands at his waist, helping him secure his belt.

She was now almost facing me, but her eyes were lowered, fixed on what she was doing. It was an awkward position to be in - one foot was still almost under her own seat, the other under the cowboy's seat, her skirt stretched tight across her spread thighs. Leaning forward, her hair was almost touching the cowboy's face. And her breasts were right in front of his eyes—I could see the soft valley of cleavage that he'd stared at earlier, and I could see how his head went dead still as he feasted his eyes.

My cock was rock hard, now. I should have been furious—on some level, I think I *was* furious. But I couldn't look away.

I think Kim had intended to fix his belt in a second or two and then step away. But of course, the belt wouldn't fasten. It was too short, and she had to spend time adjusting it before it would connect.

I knew instinctively that that wasn't an accident. The cowboy must have deliberately shortened the belt as far as it would go, just to make the process take longer. Clever. Kim stood there, her breasts swaying as she worked at the belt, jiggling right in front of his face. God, he was close enough to kiss them, if he just leaned forward a little—

I found that I was holding my breath. What the hell was wrong with me?

Kim finally fastened the belt, stepped back a little and swept her hair out of her face. Our gazes connected and she smiled at me and rolled her eyes, glancing down at the cowboy in a *what a schmuck* sort of a way, and I smiled and nodded back. Pretending that I agreed. Pretending that I was like any other, normal husband, who'd see some guy flirt with his wife and get mildly annoyed, but ultimately let it go.

But that wasn't true at all. I wasn't annoyed, on balance. There was jealousy, sure—a thick, churning sensation of wrongness in the pit of my stomach, a clutching fear that things might go further than I wanted. But both of them were more than outweighed by the arousal I felt.

As my wife took her own seat and the plane sped down the runway, I sat there stunned. I wanted the guy to check out my wife again. I wanted him to lust over her, to drool over the perfection of her body. I wanted him to get hard, imagining what he longed to do to her. I wanted—

I froze.

I'd almost thought *I want him to fuck her*. But I didn't, of course. That would be way, way too much. I wanted him to *want* to fuck her...and then I wanted to snatch her away to safety, just like the deer with the lion. I wanted the thrill of having another man chase my wife...but I wouldn't want him to actually catch her. Right?

Of course not. Jesus, what sort of man would that make me? Besides, Kim would never cheat on me, so it was academic.

My stomach lurched as the plane took off. It felt as if I was heading into a whole new world...a scary one I didn't understand, but one that beckoned me just as strongly as the beaches and bars of Jamaica. I didn't know exactly what I was feeling, but I knew I wanted more.

***

The flight to Atlanta took about four hours. I spent most of it with my eyes locked on the action four rows in front of me. I couldn't hear every word, even straining my ears, but I could make out odd phrases.

The guy didn't give up, insisting on "buying" my wife one of the complimentary drinks. She turned down his offer of wine and went for a mineral water. Part of me was proud of the fact she was so loyal, that she wouldn't even do something as harmless as accept a drink. Another part of me was almost disappointed. Why? What did I think was going to happen? That she'd have a few glasses of wine, get tipsy and allow the guy to get closer to her? Touch her? More?

I could feel my face growing hot. What was wrong with me?!

The guy's humor seemed to be wearing her down. She'd twisted in her seat to face him, her long hair tossed back over one shoulder, her arm hanging casually over the side of the seat, and he was mimicking her posture. I was sure Kim didn't think she was doing anything wrong. She *wasn't* doing anything wrong—she was just talking to the guy.

I had a better view of her now, with her twisted to the side. She was actually leaning out a bit over the aisle, which made her vest top pull tight over her breasts, the gray fabric smoothed over her soft curves. I could see the guy's gaze flick down to her chest every few seconds.

And then, abruptly, he said something and she frowned and lifted her left hand and showed it to him, her wedding band gleaming in the light from the windows. He didn't look surprised—he must have already noticed she was married—just shrugged unrepentantly. But it did shut him up. He turned to face front and picked up a magazine, my wife did the same and it was over.

***

In Atlanta, we grabbed a coffee and then boarded the connecting flight to Jamaica. This time, we had seats together. Kim smiled as she settled herself back into hers, closing her eyes. "That's sooo much better," she murmured.

I tried to sound as if I was only mildly interested. "Was is okay, sitting on your own?"

She kept her eyes closed, but a ghost of a frown crossed her face. Guilt? "It was fine. Just...you know. You can't choose who's next to you."

I played dumb, wondering if she'd mention it. "You were by some old couple, right?"

"Yeah. They were okay."

She lapsed into silence for a moment. The plane was throttling up for take-off and I sat there as the noise built, louder and louder, wondering if she was going to—

"There was this guy," she blurted, just as we started to move.

A deep throb of heat went through my groin. I tensed in my seat. "Oh?"

She sort of shrugged, eyes still closed. "Kind of an asshole." But her lips twitched in the faintest hint of a smile, and I remembered the guy's muscled chest, and his strength, and the way she'd laughed at his clowning. She sort-of liked him—that was obvious. Why was that turning me on?

"Did he bother you?" I asked. I wanted to know every detail. I wanted to know what had been going on in her head. How it had felt.

She shook her head, her golden hair tossing. "Not really. Just kind of flirting with me."

"Flirting with you?!" My excitement made me blurt it louder than I'd meant to. I sounded almost annoyed but, in reality, anger was way down the list of emotions I was feeling.

Kim's eyes flew open. "I didn't flirt back, or anything!" she said, sounding horrified. Her eyes were wide but, as I stared at her, her cheeks colored a little. She was feeling guilty, rightly or wrongly. I hadn't even considered that part of it. I'd been so fixated on the guy coming on to my wife, I hadn't really considered whether she'd done anything in response. It hadn't looked like she had, but...women can be a lot subtler than men. I remembered her tossing her hair back when she laughed. *Had* she been flirting with him, just a little?

The idea turned me on. And that, in turn, disturbed me.

I shook my head to reassure her. "I know." I paused, trying to work out what to say next. I didn't want to scare her. I sure as hell couldn't tell her about how I felt. But I was desperate to know more.

"He was just looking at me," she said. "You know, trying to get a look down my top." Perhaps subconsciously, she adjusted the vest top, tweaking the neck so that it was a little more modest. I watched, transfixed, as her breasts bounced slightly with the movement. "Typical guy."

I nodded. "Asshole."

Then I turned back to face front and started to think about ways I could make it happen again.

Victoria Kasari

CHAPTER 3

L ANDING IN MONTEGO BAY was like falling headfirst into a picture postcard. The sea was a dark, tranquil blue, lightening to a glorious pale azure as it lapped up against the white beaches. Further back rose the Blue Mountains, cool and thickly forested, the perfect counterpart to the blazing sun. As the plane taxied, I grabbed Kim's hand and squeezed hard. "I think we're going to like it here," I told her.

As soon as we'd grabbed our bags, we raced out of the terminal building. The warm air of Jamaica hit us as we finally got out of the sterile air conditioning and into the sunshine. Hotter than it had been in LA...but fresher and cleaner, too, thanks to the cool edge of the sea. I wanted to heave down huge lungfuls of it. What had happened on the plane was forgotten. Seeing the place made me remember the reason we'd come on vacation in the first place: to get closer, and fix whatever was going wrong between us.

I was so eager to get going, I practically threw our bags into the back of the cab. The cab driver, an aging black man with silver hair, threw back his head and laughed—a rich, infectious sound. "You in

Jamaica, now, mon," he told me. "You got to slow down a li'l bit."

I nodded and smiled to be polite, but I didn't pay much attention. I slipped an arm around Kim's waist and pulled her tight into me, just savoring the feeling of her against me for a moment before we climbed into the cab. This was going to be the best vacation ever.

***

Montego Bay was a riot of color and life. Even the shops themselves were painted in bright reds, yellows and greens. At first, we rushed about like all the other tourists, darting from one shop to another.

And then, slowly, the cabbie's words started to make sense. As we took a break at a roadside cafe for our first taste of Blue Mountain coffee, rich and dark and amazing, I realized something.

Everything *was* slower.

People didn't walk. They *ambled*.

I started to feel the tension drain out of me. That sense of urgency in LA that makes you dive out of bed in a panic when you realize it's past seven...that didn't exist here. We had a week to do exactly as we pleased.

I slumped back in my seat and stopped thinking about rushing to the next tourist spot. For the first time, I just...watched. And that's when I noticed how much attention Kim was getting.

There were plenty of other tourists around, of course. But we were in a huge minority. The street we were in was a little off the main streets and most people there were locals. And in Jamaica, almost everyone is black—the rich, deep mahogany of West Africa, or one of the many other subtle shades. Kim, with her softly golden skin and lustrous blonde hair, stood out. I saw heads turning, dreadlocks bouncing as men nodded their approval. Sometimes I could see their eyes and spot that gleam of lust. Some of them were wearing sunglasses and I just saw the reflection of the two of us in the lenses. But nearly all of them looked.

Kim had ditched the cardigan, now we were out of the air conditioning, and was in just her heels, blue denim skirt and gray vest top. As she leaned forward to sip her coffee, her top pulled tight over her breasts, the firm curves bulging out of the scoop neck.

Instantly, I was hard again. Not just from looking at her; from knowing others were. It was as if I was seeing my wife through new eyes: other men's eyes. All the feelings I'd had on the plane rushed back—and now, I was relaxed enough to let them spin and percolate in my mind.

I'd wanted Kim to take more risks with her clothes, to show a little more skin. I'd thought that it was because things were getting stale and predictable; I'd thought it was all about making her look different. But what if, underneath, it had been this all along? What if what I really wanted was for other men to look at her?

I gazed at her as she sat across the table, completely unaware. Should I tell her? What if she thought I was crazy, or weird? Weren't men always meant to be fiercely protective of their women, hurling guys across the bar if they so much as glanced at their girl?

What if I just did it subtly? What if I just got her to dress a little more sexily? The guy on the plane had shown that guys were already looking at her, just waiting for their chance to approach. It wouldn't take much to encourage them.

"Come on," I said, finishing off my coffee. "Let's go shopping."

***

"You have *got* to be kidding," said Kim, looking at the shirt I'd just handed her.

"Everyone's wearing them," I said. "You don't want to stand out, do you?"

We were standing in a small boutique in one of the backstreets. Ancient gold birdcages dangled from the ceiling and the air was heavy with some rich, exotic perfume. The top I'd handed Kim was a purple shirt designed to be tied under the boobs and, indeed, plenty of women in the streets were wearing something similar.

"It's too..." Kim searched for the right words. "It doesn't cover me enough."

"It's long-sleeved," I said, playing dumb. "It'll stop your arms from burning. You know how easily you burn."

Kim gave me a look. "You know what I mean. It's...." She sighed, but went to try it on.

When she emerged from the fitting room, my jaw dropped. The shirt lifted and pushed her breasts together, exposing not only the tops but the mouth-watering softness where the firm globes met, that soft valley where men dream of pushing their tongue...or their cock. If you looked down on her, you could see right down between her breasts, almost to the bottom of each one. Her bra and the fabric of the shirt kept her decent, but what was on display was heavenly. And below the knotted shirt, her midriff was left bare. She'd always kept in good shape and, never having borne a child, her stomach was trim and flat. The golden skin there was smooth and touchably soft, her navel a perfect little cave in the center.

"No," she said, looking in the mirror.

"Yes," I said firmly.

She looked round at me, surprised. "You really like it?"

"It's super-sexy."

"I don't know if I want to be super-sexy. I mean, maybe I could wear it for you in the bedroom..."

I shook my head. "We're on vacation," I reminded her. "Live a little."

***

Next was swim wear. I tried to find something along the lines of the tiny bikini I'd seen on the model in the Jamaica commercial. But, in a cool, dark swimwear store with its own mini-waterfall cascading down one wall, I found something even better.

It was a one-piece swimsuit, but it was cut daringly high on the hips and really low at the front, exposing a generous vee of her perfect breasts. The best thing, though, was the fabric. It was a dark crimson and had a high-tech, almost metallic sheen. It glistened like latex, reflecting the light and accentuating the swell of her chest, the curves of her ass. At the back, thin straps criss-crossed her back, making it look almost like a corset. It wasn't as obviously outrageous as the knotted shirt, but the thin, rubbery material clung to her like a second skin. She was covered yet, in a way, she was nude. I knew that every man on the beach would be staring at her.

And then it got even better. It was pleasantly cool in the store and, as Kim examined her back and ass in the mirror, I saw her nipples harden and begin to show through the thin fabric.

"It's kind of expensive," Kim said uncertainly, unaware of what was happening in front. "Are you sure we can—"

I slapped my credit card down on the counter in answer.

CHAPTER 4

THAT EVENING, as the sun was setting, we wandered through the streets of Montego Bay. I hadn't been able to persuade my wife into the knotted shirt, yet, but she'd slipped on a gauzy green summer dress that had a tendency to blow up around her thighs in the breeze. Combined with a pair of heels, her long legs were hard to miss.

After several drinks, we wound up in a blue-painted reggae bar right near the beach, where the party had spilled out onto the deck and from there right onto the sand. Upstairs, the balcony was filled with couples necking and men leaning over the edge, checking out the women below.

We chilled out at a small table outside for a while, and then I told Kim I had to use the restroom. It was only when I turned from her to go that I realized what I was doing: I was leaving her alone, amongst all those men. Without me there, would they just gawp at her...or would one of them approach her?

I felt my cock harden in my pants. The thought

of another guy lusting after her, maybe sitting down at the table with her....

I needed to get somewhere I could see. I could barely scramble up the stairs fast enough. It didn't help that I was sliding rapidly past tipsy and into drunk, as the wickedly potent Jamaican cocktails hit my system.

Upstairs, I made my way to the front of the balcony. There, I could look down at the tables on the deck...and at one of them was my wife, her long legs stretched lazily out in front of her. The green dress contrasted perfectly with her blonde hair and the smooth, delicate tan of her skin.

As I glanced at the rest of the deck, I caught my breath. We weren't the only white people in the bar but, from up on the balcony, it was suddenly very clear that we were in a small minority. In the fading light, my wife's skin looked very pale, adrift amidst a sea that was almost entirely black. I hadn't really considered that aspect of it before, but for some reason the sight of it sent a throb through me.

I could see the men looking at her, from tables of their own or from their little groups, glancing over their shoulders at the blonde woman sitting all alone. Some of them were on the balcony with me, looking over the edge, enjoying the view of both her legs and her cleavage.

To my disappointment, no one approached her. Probably, they'd all seen me at the table and knew I'd be back in a few minutes. I couldn't stay away long, or Kim would wonder what was wrong.

I'd just made up my mind to go down there and rejoin her when I saw him. He wasn't walking over to her—he wasn't even all that close to her. He was just leaning against a wall, a bottle of beer in his hand, taking in the scene. And yet he grabbed my attention.

The guy was big—definitely taller than me by a few inches, which would make him a full head taller than Kim. He was well built, too. A black vest showed off arms with thick swells of muscle stretching his deep brown skin. I'm not in bad shape myself, but this guy made me look small, his shoulders hulking and wide. I thought I could see tattoos on his arms, but it was difficult to see in the dim light. He wore his black hair in dreads, like many of the men, and they hung in a thick mane down over his shoulders.

It was his expression that made me stare. I could tell he was good looking—a tough face, but with a sort of feline grace that made it handsome, not brutish. He was gazing right at my wife, who seemed completely unaware of him. He didn't seem like the other men, who were practically licking their lips as they looked at her. They were like starving men eying their next meal. He was more like a connoisseur, holding a fine wine up to the light before taking the first sip. And that filled me with dread. So far, I'd felt as if I was in the position of power—the one holding the deer's rope, ready to jerk her out of harm's way. This man didn't feel like one of the lions. He felt like he was ready to snatch the rope right out of my hands and...

...and take her for himself.

Energy seemed to crackle through my body, leaving me breathless and almost panting. It was crazy, of course. No one was going to run off with Kim. I was just having fun, showing off my wife and watching other men's reactions.

Something dark and hot seemed to twist and squirm inside me. Was that all I wanted? Just to see their reactions? Tease them and then pull her away? Or did I want to see it go further than that? Did I want to see their hands on her body?

That last thought made me grip the balcony's handrail, my knuckles white, in mixed lust and fear. I looked down at the dreadlocked man beneath, lounging so confidently against the wall. I stared at his huge hand, wrapped around the beer bottle, and I imagined it closing around Kim's soft shoulder, pushing her back in her seat as he pressed up against her and—

I swallowed. Suddenly, I was imagining his lips on hers, his tongue thrusting into her mouth. His hands mauling her breasts, lifting her summer dress up around her hips. Shoving her up against a wall, his fingers grabbing her panties—

I broke and ran through the crowd. For the first time since all this had started on the plane, I was scared. Something about that man was different. Something about him made me deeply uneasy...and yet, at the same time, the thought of him with my wife, even *near* my wife, had my cock harder than it had ever been.

As I pounded down the stairs, there was one image I couldn't get out of my head. His black, naked body entwined with hers. Spreading her. Pushing his way into her.

I burst out of the bar and stumbled through the crowd, expecting to see the guy leaning over our table, talking to her, or with his hands already on her. But Kim sat alone.

My head snapped round to look at the wall where he'd been standing. But he was gone. I looked around, but I couldn't see him in the crowd anywhere, either.

"Honey?" Kim was frowning at me. "You okay?"

I swallowed. I didn't know what to say. I didn't even know what was going on in my own head. I'd been terrified...and yet incredibly turned on.

"No restroom," I managed at last. "There's no

restroom here. Let's head to a different bar."

As we left, I couldn't help turning back to scan the crowd for the guy, but he was still nowhere to be found. That should have been a relief...so why did I feel almost disappointed?

***

On the walk back to the hotel, I calmed down. I told myself there'd been plenty of other guys who'd been looking at Kim, some of them much more obviously than he had. That was what I'd wanted, right? Men to lust after her. What was different about that one guy, that he caused real fear as well as even greater excitement?

Halfway back, I figured it out. It was his potential. The other guys would look, maybe flirt, maybe a little more. But there was something serious about that one guy, as if he played for keeps. Or as if, with him, it wouldn't be a game at all.

I resolved that, if I ever saw him again, I'd keep Kim well away from him. And yet, at the same time, I couldn't get him out of my head.

Back in our hotel room, I wandered over to the window for a moment and stood there, trying to get a handle on things. I was horny. I was scared—as much by what was going on in my own head as by what had actually happened. Had I always felt like this? Had I always enjoyed the idea of men looking at my wife, and just never known it...or never admitted it?

I heard Kim move in behind me. A second later, I felt the press of her breasts against my back.

That was new. We'd barely had sex in weeks, and even then it hadn't been her that had initiated things. It was time to get back to *us,* and forget about selfish fantasies.

I turned around and looked down at her. She'd slipped off her heels, so she had to tilt her chin up to look at me. *If I was him,* I thought, *that dreadlocked guy, she'd have to look up even* in *heels.*

I blinked. Where had *that* come from? I shook my head to clear it and put my hands on her waist. Then I leaned down and kissed her.

One of the things I love most about my wife is the feel of her lips. Silky and soft and, when she's turned on, her mouth has this way of just slowly flowering open under your mouth, and she gives this soft little moan. She did it for me right then, her eyes fluttering closed, and I slid my tongue into her mouth, feeling its softness. We started to kiss, at first slowly and then open-mouthed and hungry, our heads beginning to move as our mouths explored each other. My hands slid up over her back, then down to the ripe curves of her ass. She slipped her arms around me, her fingers tracing my shoulders, my back, then over my chest, her palms warm through my shirt.

We finally broke for air. Kim's eyes were sparkling. "*Wow!*" she said. "We haven't kissed like that in—"

"Weeks," I said.

"*Forever,*" she told me, and grabbed the back of my head and pulled me in again. This time, my hands roved over her sides, then slid up over her trim stomach to cup her breasts, gently squeezing them. I felt her start to move under my hands, a slow, sinuous flexing as she started to grind against my touch. When we broke apart, she was panting. "We have to come on vacation more often!" she said, grinning.

I blinked at that. I'd been just as horny back

home...hadn't I? I'd thought it was her that hadn't been interested. Had it been both of us, and I just hadn't been aware of it?

Well, no matter. I was sure as hell horny now. I pushed her back towards the bed.

"It must be the sun," she said, as she let herself fall back onto the bed. The summer dress flapped up around her thighs and she made no attempt to tug it down again. "Or the heat. Or just being away."

I was smiling, too. She was right—I hadn't felt this good in months...maybe years. We really had needed a vacation. "Yeah," I told her. "It's the weather and the open air and seeing—"

I bit back my words. I'd almost said, *and seeing men looking at you.*

"Seeing what?" asked Kim, still grinning.

I couldn't tell her—of course not. That was weird, right, wanting to see other guys lusting after your wife? "Seeing you...dressed so sexy," I said. And leaned down and kissed her neck.

She squirmed under me in delight and then looked down at the sundress. "Really? This old thing?" Then her eyes narrowed, but in a teasing way. "Or did you mean that purple shirt you bought me?"

I looked down at her beautiful breasts, remembering how they'd looked in the shirt. "God, yes," I said breathlessly. I fell on her, my lips tracing a path down her collarbone and then down to the upper slopes of her breasts. She moaned long and low in her throat, then again as I cupped her breasts. Her body was just perfect—exactly the right combination of soft and firm, her breasts squashing under my kisses but rolling up to meet my lips, full and weighty in my hands.

The summer dress was held up by a couple of flimsy shoulder straps. I tugged them down over her shoulders along with her bra straps, jerking the fabric from underneath her, and a second later her breasts were bared, golden skin and delicate pink nipples. I feasted my eyes for a second before taking one in my mouth. Her skin was so smooth under my tongue, and as I lapped at the firmer flesh of her nipples I could feel them tighten and harden in my mouth.

"Do you want me to wear it?" she said, and it was almost a groan. She arched her back, thrusting her breasts into my face. "I can put it on right now. Though we've kinda moved past that point."

I was barely thinking. "No," I said, lifting my mouth off her for a second. "Out."

Damn! Why had I said that? I didn't want her to have any clue as to what I was thinking. Maybe she wouldn't notice.

But Kim was way too smart for that. "Out? Why do you want me to—Oh God, keep doing that!—Why do you want me to wear it out?"

I kept licking, moving my mouth from one breast to the other while I lifted and cupped and rolled them in my hands. My cock was stiff and hot against my thigh and everything felt so good...I really hoped I hadn't given the game away.

But, when I finally lifted my head, leaving her breasts shining wetly, she was still frowning slightly, gazing up at me. She was just as turned on as me, but she still wanted an answer.

I sort of shrugged. "I don't know. It's more fun, I guess, if everyone can see you." I tried to keep my voice light, as if it wasn't at all important. My hands slid under the skirt of her dress, moving up her thighs and pushing the dress up at the same time.

"Everyone?" She looked down at my rising hands, gasping as my palms passed over her knees, her thighs, her upper thighs. "You mean...other guys?"

I only glanced up at her, just for a second. But something in my expression must have given me away.

"You like other guys looking at me?" she asked slowly.

I had the waistband of her panties—soft, cotton blue ones—hooked around my fingers. I shrugged, trying to focus very intently on what I was doing so that I didn't look her in the eye again. "I don't know. Maybe. I guess. Sometimes." I slid her panties down her legs and off, then pushed her dress right up to her waist so that I could see her.

She hadn't really caught any sun, yet, so there were no tan lines. Her whole body was that gorgeous, softly golden tone, the perfect counterpoint to her long, blonde hair. And right up between her thighs, gleaming in the room's mood lights, was the other piece of blonde hair—the one that all the men longed to see, the one they wondered about when they saw the hair on her head. The one that proved she was indeed a natural blonde.

Kim waxed herself almost smooth, keeping just a narrow strip of hair above her pussy lips—enough to be glimpsed, on the rare occasions she wore sheer lingerie in the bedroom, or when I saw her completely naked. I found it even sexier than if she was completely smooth there, and she knew it. Beneath the golden hair, her outer lips were softly pink and already swollen and slightly plump with her desire. I knew that if I started to rub at them, she'd open to me almost instantly. I knew that I'd find her wet inside. I could see the tell-tale flush in her cheeks. But, as I locked eyes with her for a second, I could see that I hadn't gotten away with it. She still wanted a straight answer.

"You like other guys looking at me?" she asked again.

I gently pushed her thighs apart, and she didn't resist. The sight of her pussy slowly opening to me, the outer lips just barely parting, was one of the most beautiful things I'd ever seen. I leaned down and just breathed on her, letting my hot breath play across her sensitive flesh, and she gasped. Then I started to trace her lips with my tongue. Almost as soon as I touched her, the lips were easing apart, her wetness obvious. I eased a finger inside her, amazed at how slick she was. *She really is just as horny as I am.*

I started to lick at her clit, teasing it until I could feel it swollen and throbbing beneath its soft hood. I heard Kim's hands dig hard into the bedclothes, clutching the fabric in her fists. She'd gone quiet, now, giving herself up to the sensations as I added a second finger. She let out a hiss of pleasure as I slid them deep, then hooked them to touch that secret spot. I rubbed gently, barely a touch on her satin-smooth flesh, but with my tongue on her clit at the same time, it was enough to make her roll and grind her hips, her breathing quickening into short, hard pants.

She stepped her feet apart on the bed, raising her knees. Welcoming me in.

I pulled back onto my knees and scrabbled at my belt, shoving my pants off and pulling my shirt over my head. Kim was still semi-dressed, her dress and bra pushed down below her breasts, the skirt up around her hips. I don't think she'd ever looked sexier.

I took my cock in my hand, guiding it to her. My cock is about average, I guess—certainly, Kim's never complained. Rock hard and throbbing, the head approached her shining pussy lips.

"Wait," she said, grabbing my arm. "Condom."

I hesitated. We were planning on trying for a baby anyway later that year. Would it hurt to start a little sooner? But she was right—we were the sort of couple who planned everything. We'd wait until we were fully ready.

I grabbed a condom from my bag and rolled it on, then raced back to the bed. She lay there looking up at me, her breathing quick, her face flushed. I started to guide my cock into her, nudging the soft folds apart with the very tip, savoring the sensation of penetrating her. She felt amazing, hot and tight, even through the rubber barrier.

I was halfway inside when she said, "You do like it, don't you? Other guys looking at me?"

It was impossible to lie. I didn't even have to say anything. The answer was all over my face. I felt my cheeks go hot.

But she didn't look angry, exactly. She looked...cautious.

I planted my hands either side of her head and slid slowly deeper. The hot tightness of her made it difficult to think.

"Why?" she asked as I hilted myself.

I stopped there for a moment and, as I answered, I could feel myself stiffen even more. I could actually feel myself swelling as I said the words. "I like them all...wanting you."

I started to draw myself out of her, slow and steady. She was like honey and satin around me.

"Wanting to fuck me?" she asked suddenly.

I almost lost it right then. I swear my cock actually jerked in response, and I'm sure she felt it. "Yes," I croaked. "God, yes."

The tiniest of smiles appeared on her lips. "You want them all thinking about me. Imagining what they're going to do to me."

I lowered myself onto my forearms, until her nipples grazed my chest, and started to move. "Yes!"

She stared up at me in silence for a few minutes as my pace built, her hips building into a rhythm of their own as she ground and swirled them against me.

"You want them hot for me," she said at last. "Until they can't help themselves—"

"Yes!" I panted. My thrusts sped up.

"You want them to pull my dress up—"

My eyes widened, but I didn't stop thrusting. I was hammering into her now, the bed creaking and protesting.

"—and rip my panties off and just shove it inside me, and fuck me up against the wall—"

I couldn't believe what was coming out of her mouth. "Yes!" I said in a strangled voice, "God, yes!" My hips were savage between her thighs, pounding my cock into her.

"—and I'm looking over his shoulder at you as he fucks me—"

I felt her come, then, faster than she'd ever reached her peak before. And the feeling of her squeezing and clutching around me—or more likely her words—sent me over the edge. I felt myself shoot long hot ropes of cum into the condom, and then she was straining her head up to meet mine and we were kissing, our tongues intertwining.

When I finally lifted myself off her and rolled to the side, she let out a long breath. "Well," she said. "That was...."

Cold reality started to set in: my secret was exposed. I looked across at her, terrified. She had that cautious look in her eyes but, as before, she didn't look angry. In fact, she looked...

embarrassed. It hit me that she'd been just as into it as I had.

"This is...new," I said tentatively.

She nodded, flushing. But then smiled. We lay there in silence for a moment, neither one wanting to go first.

"I don't want to sleep with anyone else," she said at last. Almost defensively.

"God, no!" I said quickly. "Of course not!"

"I mean, it's just a fantasy, right?" she asked, her eyes wide. "You don't really want me to—"

"No!"

"You're sure?"

"Yes! No, I definitely don't want you to sleep with another guy." As I said it, though, as the words *sleep with another guy* left my lips, I felt my cock jerk. A sudden image of her, on her back on a bed, with a stranger between her legs. One with long, black dreadlocks.

I pushed the thought from my mind. Of *course* it was just a fantasy!

She turned fully onto her side and drew me to her, and we cuddled, her head on my shoulder. The warmth of her body felt good—reassuring. "It turned you on as well, though," I said. "Didn't it?"

She hesitated. I could imagine her cheeks turning bright red. Then she nodded. "Is that bad?"

"No! I mean, how can it be bad, if I like it, too?"

We lapsed into silence again. Her breasts were soft against my chest, her long hair trailing down over my shoulder. The fact we weren't looking into each other's eyes anymore made me a little braver. I didn't want to lose the moment.

"So you like them looking at you?" I asked.

I felt her nod.

"Would you like...to do it some more?"

She drew back from me and, for a second, I

thought I'd blown it. But she just looked suspiciously into my eyes. "What do you mean, 'do it'? They're looking at me. Isn't it something *they* do?"

"But you could dress sexy. And we could go where the men are."

She sort of squirmed. "You mean...tease them?"

"Yes. Tease them."

She thought about it. "That might be fun."

I pulled her to me and hugged her. I had the best wife in the world.

CHAPTER 5

W E SPENT the next day by the pool. The hotel had an infinity pool that made it feel as if you were swimming in the open ocean and, with the sun warming the water and waiters bringing us cold drinks, it was idyllic. There was plenty of eye candy—all around me were women in swimsuits and bikinis. But none of them were as beautiful as my wife.

Neither of us mentioned what had happened the night before. I hadn't even tried to get Kim to wear the new metallic red swimsuit I'd bought her. The whole thing might as well have been a dream.

Until the evening.

As we dressed to go out, Kim asked me, "Um...do you want me to wear the purple shirt?"

I turned and looked at her and she met my eyes. And I knew she was asking about more than just the outfit.

"Yes," I said, my heart already beating faster. "That'd be great."

When it was on, the shirt looked even better than I'd remembered it. Even with a bra, she looked as if she really was in danger of her boobs escaping from the shirt's snug embrace. With the bare midriff, too, there was a lot of skin on display. I actually started to feel a little nervous, now that we were actually doing this. Did I really want every guy gawping at my wife?

And then I remembered the feeling of watching them. Their hungry stares. Yes, I definitely did want it.

Kim put on a black, clingy skirt. Not too short—it finished a little above the knee. But it showed off the ripe curves of her ass superbly. She added a pair of heels, a little higher than she'd usually wear, and they made her already long legs look even longer. The effect, when added together, was—

"Stunning," I told her. "You look stunning."

She walked up to me and pressed up against me, her breasts pillowing against my chest. I slid my hands all the way down her—mostly naked—back and clutched her ass through the skirt. The fabric was so thin and tight that I could feel the muscles of her ass cheeks as she shifted her weight. "I'm not done yet," she told me.

She broke away from me and did her make-up. Then she blow dried and straightened her hair. When she turned around I let out an audible gasp.

With her honey-blonde hair glass-straight, everything about her looked sleek, sexy and glossy: her exposed tan cleavage, her long legs and her wetly-glossed lips. She was wearing more eyeliner and mascara than usual. Not too much—it was classy, not slutty. But it made her eyes look bigger and more seductive. She was going to turn the head of any man who saw her.

And I was going to make sure that they saw her. Instead of keeping her safe home for myself, I was going to parade her in public, encouraging the men to pant and slather for her, before pulling her to safety. A twang of guilt hit me. Was this right? What sort of a man did this?

But she'd go home with *me*, and the sex afterwards would be amazing.

I kissed her, barely having to bend down—in the new heels, she was only a few inches smaller than me. "Let's do this," I said.

***

I'd thought a good deal about where to take her and had looked through the tourist guides to find the bars that would be full. Once we were on the main tourist streets, though, it was easy—we just followed the sound of thumping music and looked for the places that were full of people. We'd deliberately waited until almost eleven to head out, to ensure everywhere would be busy.

We headed for a packed bar not far away, where the music throbbed through the windows and the crowd seemed to be our age. As we got closer, Kim squeezed my hand.

"Still want to do this?" I asked.

She nodded. A second later, as we passed through the doors and into the dark, blue-lit interior, she gave another little excited squeeze.

It was cooler inside and, with the main light coming from about a thousand tiny blue LEDs in the ceiling, it felt almost as if we were underwater. People were lounging on white beanbags with cold beers, or standing around at the bar drinking cocktails. At first, it felt like everyone was black, but when I looked more carefully there were quite a few white tourists there as well—though only about ten percent of the crowd.

As we passed through the crowd, I could see

male heads turning to look at her. The heels made her ass sway as she walked and I saw the men's hungry looks as they watched those firm cheeks go back and forth. I knew what was going through their minds because it was going through my mind, too. They were imagining grabbing her ass with both hands, fondling those firm cheeks and then pushing up against her, stroking their hardening cocks in the cleft between the half-moons, until it was achingly erect. Then pushing her forward against the bar, making her bend over it to present her ass even more readily. The black skirt would be tugged up, exposing her. Her panties would be ripped off. And then, as she moaned in pleasure—

I drew in my breath, feeling the rising lust in the crowd around me. It was like a physical heat around us, pressing inward. I walked Kim over to the bar and ordered a couple of beers.

I saw the bartender—a guy in his thirties with a gleaming silver ring through one ear—do a double-take as Kim came up to the bar and leaned against it. Her breasts were already wantonly displayed by the purple shirt, but when she leaned forward a little, her nipples were almost exposed. I saw his hands shake as he passed us the two frosty bottles, his eyes firmly fixed on Kim's chest. He barely remembered to ask me for the money.

I could feel the eyes of the crowd on our backs. Then I realized there was a mirror above the bar and, glancing casually up at it, I saw just how many of the men were eying Kim up. Some of them were doing it openly, while others were taking sneaky peeks over their shoulders, now that they thought we couldn't see. Several huddles of men were talking in low voices, too low to be heard over the music even if I could have understood the Jamaican patois. But from the way they kept glancing at Kim, nudging each other and smiling, I knew the sorts of things they were saying: discussing her body; rating her, maybe, on a scale of ten—surely, she'd rate at least a nine; talking about what they wanted to do to her...or what they wanted her to do to them.

Another ripple of guilt went through me. Was this right? They shouldn't be thinking those things...not about my wife! In their minds, she was already kneeling in front of them, her mouth open, her hand reaching for their cocks....

The heat flared up inside me, banishing the guilt. Not that I'd ever want anything like that to happen, not in reality. But knowing that they were thinking it...that was amazing.

"Do you think they're looking at me?" asked Kim nervously. It took me completely by surprise.

"God, yes! Can you not feel it? They're all looking at you!"

"Really?" She smiled a little, and there was a hint of a blush. I realized that it wasn't being looked at that was making her nervous. It was fear that maybe no one would look.

"Honey, you're *gorgeous*. Every man here wants you. Every one of them. Look in the mirror."

I saw her take a breath and then glance up— and immediately her eyes widened. She quickly dropped her eyes again, but now she was breathing fast. "God...they really are!" She smiled a little wider, as if loving it but ashamed.

"That's not new, you know," I said slowly. "Men are always looking at you, back in LA. Even when you don't dress up."

She looked at me sharply, a doubting look on her face.

I blinked at her. "Did you really not know?" I asked, amazed. I'd never even considered that she might not realize how stunning she was. I was always telling her she was beautiful.

But then it hit me: me telling her that she was beautiful wasn't the same as other men lusting after her. Maybe she didn't trust my opinion anymore—she knew that I loved her, after all. Maybe she thought I'd lie, just to make her feel good. But another man lusting after her...that was an objective opinion and totally unknown territory. Would I be willing to do the same—to dress up in something designed to show me off, and encourage a room full of women to stare...to judge me?

I suddenly understood why she didn't dress up sexily at home. And also how brave she was being, doing it now. I grinned. "I love you," I blurted. "You know that, right?"

She smiled, too. She was still nervous, but her eyes were shining—she had a kind of glow, one I hadn't seen in a long time. The last hint of guilt died away. Tonight could be a good thing for her—and for *us*. It was giving her confidence of a sort that a million *you look great, honey*'s from me never could. I leaned in and kissed her, relishing the softness of her lips, the sweet smell of her perfume. I could feel her warm breasts pushing against my arm as she nestled closer, and the kiss went on and on.

When we moved apart, we were both grinning like loons. "This was a good idea," she told me, and I nodded.

I sipped some beer, and it was only when I glanced in the mirror again that I realized everything had changed. All the men who'd been looking at Kim were looking away, now. Occasionally, they'd look her way, but it was just a passing glance.

They knew. They knew we were married. I mean, I guessed with hindsight that much had been obvious, since we'd walked in together. Maybe they'd even noticed our wedding rings. But the kiss had been the final straw. The beautiful blonde who'd strolled into their bar was clearly very, very taken.

I wouldn't have changed anything, though. The revelation I'd had was worth any amount of men lusting after Kim. I was more than happy.

When we left, though, hand in hand, I felt the stirrings of lust. Back on the street, amongst men who hadn't seen us in the bar, there was more interest. As an experiment, I casually dropped her hand when we were halfway down the street and just walked side-by-side. The number of men checking her out definitely went up.

They had to think she was single. That was the next step.

I knew she wouldn't have agreed to it before, but now that she was feeling more confident....

"Are you enjoying it?" I asked, taking her hand again for reassurance.

She nodded and blushed. "Yeah. I feel like maybe I shouldn't. I mean, I shouldn't *need* other men looking at me...."

I shrugged. "Why not? It doesn't bother me—in fact, the opposite. You know that. We all need...I don't know...approval?"

She nodded. "So what now? Go into another bar?" I was surprised by how enthusiastic she sounded. I'd been worried that I'd persuaded her into this but, now that she'd tried it, she seemed at least as eager as me.

It crossed my mind that that didn't matter. Just because we both wanted to do it, didn't make it right...or safe. Something could still go wrong with this whole game, and it would still be me who'd started it.

But what was going to go wrong?

"Maybe we could go a little further," I said carefully. "Like...what if you went into the next place on your own?"

"On my own?!"

"I'd be right there with you...just a minute behind, so it doesn't look like we're together."

She thought about it. "And then what?"

"You take a seat at the bar, order a drink...or wait for someone to buy you one."

"You think they'll do that?"

"Of course they'll do that. It'll be a race to see who gets to you first."

She bit her lip, thinking. "And then what?"

"Maybe you talk to a guy. Let him flirt with you a bit."

She did one of her little squirms—just a tiny shimmy of her spine, but it let me know that she was both turned on and slightly disturbed by the idea. Or, more likely, disturbed *because* she was turned on by it. "Flirt? But no touching?"

I stopped walking. I hadn't thought that far ahead. "I don't know," I said honestly.

She stopped too, and turned to me. "Do you want him to touch me?" she asked in a low voice.

We both stood there staring at each other, both of us wearing poker faces. Neither of us seemed to want to speak first.

Touching her? I hadn't really thought about that. I mean, I had thought about it in my fantasies—I'd gone much further than that, in my fantasies—but having another man's hands on her in real life? Was I ready for that?

"Maybe?" I said at last, hedging my bets. "A little?"

She swallowed and nodded.

"I mean, are you okay with that?" I asked.

50

"Because that's what's important. Are you okay with it?"

She nodded again. She looked very serious, and I was worried for a moment that I'd offended her. Then I saw how fast she was breathing. She wasn't angry; she was turned on. "Okay," she said. "But how do we...I mean, how do we end things? Do you come over and tell him I'm with you?"

In a way, that appealed to me. Snatching her away from under their noses, just as they thought they were getting somewhere. But, at the same time, I wasn't doing this to humiliate them. Better to leave them feeling good about the beautiful blonde they met. Then we'd all be having fun, and no harm would be done to anyone.

At that stage, it all still felt perfectly safe.

There was another reason, too. Assuming we did this more than once, maybe some of these guys who met Kim would talk to each other. It was a long shot, but the idea that one guy might tell his pal about the gorgeous blonde American he met in a bar, and his friend saying that he thought he'd met her too, and then comparing notes on her breasts, her ass, her smile...that made me go heady with lust.

"I'll signal you," I said, starting to walk again. "I'll be in the bar, but the guy won't know you're with me. So you can keep an eye on me and when I signal you, you make your excuses and leave."

Kim's face lit up. "A signal? Like a secret signal, like we're spies?"

I grinned. "Yeah."

She smiled. "I always wanted to be a spy. You could scratch your ear or something."

Then it hit me that we were missing something obvious. "Wait. Do you have your phone with you?"

She did, of course. Kim and her phone were

inseparable. We arranged that I'd call her when I wanted it to end, or if it looked like things were going too far, and if she needed an escape route before that, she'd look in her handbag and that would be my cue to call her early. "I'll pretend you're my friend, back at the hotel," Kim told me. "And you've got food poisoning. And I have to come and look after you."

I blinked. "That's good," I said. "You would have made a good spy."

I saw another bar at the end of the street. A big place, with plenty of people in it. Perfect. "Ready to try it?" I asked.

She bit her lip. "I don't know. Wait. So I'm a single woman sitting at the bar? Do people even do that?"

"Sure. I mean, if you're single, what else are you going to do?" Thinking about it, back in the days I used to hit the bars as a single guy, most girls were there in groups. Did women really go to bars and sit there on their own, waiting for someone to notice them? What sort of women?

Women who were looking for a man. That's the message Kim would be sending. She might as well hang a sign around her neck saying *single and looking*. The thought sent a wave of heat down my body, ending in a tightening of my cock. "You'll be fine," I told her. Then I remembered something. "Wait! Your ring. Take your ring off."

She looked horrified. "Take my *ring* off?!"

"Otherwise they'll know you're married."

She looked doubtfully at her wedding band. "That feels...wow. That's a big thing."

She stood there staring at it for so long that I changed my mind. I didn't want to upset her. "Forget it," I said.

But she abruptly shook her head. "No. You're

right. If we're going to play this game, let's play it properly." And she slid off her wedding band. She swallowed. "Wow. God, that feels weird." She looked at her engagement ring. "This, too?"

I shrugged nervously. "I guess. Unless you want to pretend you're someone's fiancée who's cheating?"

Her eyes went wide. "I don't want him to think I'm cheating!" She looked up at me, worried. "*This* isn't cheating, is it? I mean, should we even be doing this?"

I put my hand on her shoulder. "No. It's not cheating. How can it be cheating if we both want it? It's fine."

She nodded slowly and slid the diamond ring from her finger, then stared at the bare digit. "God. That's the first time they've been off since they went on. It feels...wow. I didn't think it'd feel this weird."

I stared at her hand. Luckily, the rings had been loose enough that there wasn't a noticeable tan line. There was nothing to suggest she was married. It made her look...different. More than you'd think a tiny bit of metal could. She wasn't a married woman anymore. She was young, beautiful...and available.

"Don't lose them," she said, a nervous lilt in her voice, and laid the rings in my palm. I put them carefully into my deepest pocket.

Kim stared at the door of the bar, as much fear as excitement on her face. "Don't panic," I said gently. "I'll be right there with you, just a little way behind."

She nodded. And then, shoulders set, she walked off ahead of me. I watched her all the way to the door, heads already turning as she passed men in the street. At the door, she hesitated for a moment, then stepped inside and disappeared into

the darkness.
    And it began.

CHAPTER 6

I STOOD OUTSIDE for a moment, wondering how long to wait. *We should have talked about that.* One minute? Two? I didn't want it to look as if we'd just been briefly separated, and I was chasing after her. I wanted her to have enough time to get to the bar and sit down. On the other hand, if I waited too long, she might think I'd abandoned her.

And what if something happened to her? The guilt came back. I'd just sent my wife, alone and scantily dressed, into a bar neither of us knew, at close to midnight. I stared at the dark doorway. What if I went inside and she was already gone? What if some guy had pulled her into the restrooms? What if she was being dragged, a hand over her mouth, out of the bar and into a dark alley...or into the back of a van, never to be seen again?

I told myself I was being ridiculous. We were right in the heart of the tourist area, and she was in a public place. Nothing was going to happen to her.

Even so, after two minutes I couldn't wait any longer. My breath tight in my chest, I strode down the street and into the bar.

Inside, it took my eyes a few minutes to adjust to the gloom. The place was one big room, with a live band playing reggae on a stage at one end. In the middle, there was a crowd of people standing around watching and drinking. At the far end was the bar, with a line of cherry red bar stools.

My heart stopped. Kim wasn't there.

Wait: *there!* My heart started beating again as a guy moved aside and I saw her. She was sitting diagonally on a bar stool, her bare knees almost touching—

I drew in my breath. There was already a guy sitting next to her, talking to her. Jesus, he must have pounced the instant she walked in!

It was difficult to judge his age, but I pegged him at a few years younger than me. Black, like almost everyone in the place, with his hair in tight cornrows. His bright orange shirt would have looked ridiculous on me but, against his brown-black skin, I had to admit it looked great. He was wearing khaki cargo pants and sandals, like he'd just stepped in off the beach. As he leaned in closer to talk to Kim, everything about him said *casual*. Easy-going. I was too far away to hear what he was saying, but I saw him point down the street, then off in the other direction. As if he was telling her about nearby places. Definitely a local, then. That was probably his chat-up shtick: helping the poor white tourist who doesn't know her way around. I wondered if he was going to offer to show her the sights.

His shirt was open a few buttons at his neck, showing off smooth, dark skin and a hint of broad, curving pecs. He had that "X"-shaped body woman go nuts for—big chest and narrow waist, then powerful thighs. Not as big—or as good looking, I decided—as the guy I'd seen from the balcony the night before. But still obviously a guy who could pick and choose.

And tonight, he'd chosen my wife.

Kim was playing her part, her bare knees almost touching him as she sat there, drink in one hand, body leaning in to him slightly. Her expression was captivated, a broad smile on her face. I could see the guy grinning, too, his eyes locked on hers...except when they flicked down to that smooth, perfect cleavage. God, she looked so beautiful—every guy in the bar must be wishing for a better look at those breasts, those legs. Wishing they were the lucky guy at the bar with her. And if they noticed me at all, they must think I was just like them, another competitor who'd gotten there too late.

I moved closer, planting myself against a wall and then edging along it, as if I was trying to find a spot to lean and chill. I tried to keep my eyes moving around the bar so that it wasn't obvious I was staring at the couple, but it was hard to tear my gaze from them.

The couple. That's how I'd thought of them, for a second. That's how everyone else would see them. Anyone entering the bar now would spot my wife and then see the man talking to her and know that she was taken...but not by *me*. The idea sent a strange shudder through me—not unlike fear, but ending in a hot wave that soaked straight down to my groin.

The guy shuffled closer on his bar stool—only an inch, but it made all the difference. Now, when he leaned in to tell her something, he could—yes—

touch her on the shoulder without looking as if he was reaching. He made out that it was a casual touch, but I saw my wife stiffen...then relax. That was the first contact, the breaking down of the first of her barriers. And once he'd gotten her comfortable with that...

As I stared at them sitting there together, his black hand so close to her lightly tan skin, the difference between them really hit me for the first time. It hadn't even occurred to me until I'd seen Kim back in the other bar, the only white woman in a sea of black men. But now it was becoming obvious that, whoever we randomly pulled into our little game, he was almost certainly going to be black. And somehow, the idea of Kim being lusted after...flirted with...*touched* by a black guy was even hotter than if a white guy was doing it. I couldn't figure out why. Something about the look of his dark skin against her much paler flesh was just so intoxicating, so erotic. God, imagine if they were naked, his black body between her white thighs—

I cut off that train of thought. That wasn't going to happen, of course. We wouldn't go anywhere near that far.

The man looked over his shoulder, as if afraid of being overheard by someone. Then he beckoned her closer and they leaned their heads together. His heavyset jaw was suddenly right up against her ear as he whispered to her. She giggled, then laughed loudly, a musical sound. And his hand was suddenly on her back, as if to help her lean in to him. But the hand rubbed in slow circles, over her back...her lower back...and then his fingers were just skimming over her ass. I saw her stiffen again...and relax again.

I wasn't sure how I felt about that. The sight of his hand there made my face go hot in anger and shame but, at the same time, I could feel my cock throb and grow. God...that was my *wife!* My wife he had his hand on, the fingertips stroking and exploring. Her skirt was so thin that she might as well be naked...he'd be able to feel every firm curve of her, feel the warmth of her skin through the material. And I was standing by and letting it happen. No, *making* it happen!

I put one hand in my pocket, feeling the comforting shape of my phone. I could end this. At any moment, I could end this.

But I didn't want to.

Then the guy half-got up and moved his bar stool closer to hers, so they were almost touching. When he sat next to her again, their thighs were pressed together, and I imagined the heat of her against him. Kim glanced around for a second, maybe looking for me, but she didn't seem to see me. I could see that her face was flushed, though, her eyes wide with arousal.

The guy's arm slipped around her waist, his hand curling around her to snug her in close to him. Their faces were inches apart now. God, was he going to kiss her? We hadn't talked about kissing!

He was staring very intensely into her eyes, now, as he spoke in a slow voice. I wished I could hear what he was saying, but the music from the band was too loud.

He said something and Kim's mouth fell open...and then I saw, quite clearly, her gaze drop to the front of his pants. Then he took her hand in his and glanced towards the door.

He was trying to get her to leave with him! Would she do it? What would happen if she did? I imagined a seedy hotel room, or even the two of them going back to *our* hotel room. The two of them on the bed, him stripping her clothes from her, his mouth and hands ravishing her naked body, then his pants dropping to the floor—

My fingers closed around my phone, but they froze there. For a second, I actually hesitated.

Then I pulled it out and hit the quick-dial icon for Kim. Long seconds passed while the call connected and then, to my relief, Kim gave a little jerk and looked down at her purse, then pulled out her phone and answered.

"Are you okay?" I asked without thinking. "Don't leave with him!"

"Really?" said Kim. "God, you're throwing up? That's awful! I'll be right there!" And she hung up.

Over at the bar, I saw her talk quickly to the guy and get up from her stool. The guy looked a little disgruntled, but nodded and took the opportunity to savor the view of her chest, now at eye level, as he sat there.

Seconds later, Kim bustled out of the bar. I held back for a minute so that it wouldn't look too obvious, then followed.

Kim was waiting just outside. She was pacing around, grinning crazily, almost giggling. I grabbed her hand and towed her down the street. "Tell me everything!" I said breathlessly.

She pushed in close against me, nestling against my body. Closer than normal, in fact. Maybe she wanted to reassure me that she was still mine. "His name was Thomas," she told me. "He works on one of the tourist boats."

"He had his hand on your ass."

"I know." She grinned. "It felt good."

Rage bubbled up inside me and I went quiet for a moment. We walked in tense silence. Until now, the jealousy had been overshadowed by my arousal and I'd only felt it distantly, like a storm you can see on the horizon. Now, though, it was right on top of me. "Okay," I said, in a voice that betrayed that it wasn't.

She looked at me, worried. I could see the fear in her eyes, then—that she'd hurt me. "Does it bother you? We can stop—"

"No," I said quickly. The jealousy was still there. The thought that another man had given her pleasure, that his hand had been on her body.... But those were the exact same things that turned me on so much. The anger and lust were like two sides of the same coin. I couldn't have one without the other. "No, it's...."

She waited patiently for a reply.

I tried to find the right words. "It's...part of it? I think?" I said at last. "I am enjoying it. Definitely." I swallowed. "How did it feel?" My insides were twisting. Would she think I was weird?

"It felt different," she told me. "Different to you."

"Why?" I asked hoarsely.

"Because it was someone new, I think. You remember what it's like to kiss someone for the first time, or touch them for the first time? All the excitement. Not sure if it's going to happen or not. It was that."

I was trying to remember what it had been like, back in the early days with Kim. Going on dates, imagining what she looked like under her blouse, then getting her down to her bra and imagining her nipples. Each time, we'd go a little further. Would this be the night I got to feel her breasts? Her pussy? Fuck her? God, it had been incredible. And just now, Thomas had had all that with my wife...and she'd had it with him.

"And also..." Kim was saying, "I think because...." She flushed.

"Because he was black?" I asked quietly.

She hesitated, then nodded guiltily.

"Have you ever...been with a black guy before? Maybe before we met?"

She shook her head. "I think that's part of it. That I've never...." She trailed off. "Does it make me racist?"

I pulled her closer. "I don't think so. I'm pretty sure it didn't bother Thomas, if it turned you on that he was black."

"He was just so...*different,* you know? Different to any guy I'd had before."

I nodded. I'd been feeling something similar, watching the two of them together. "What about at the end? It looked like he wanted you to go somewhere with him."

She smirked. "He told me that he was hard for me."

My eyes bugged out. I remembered her looking at his groin.

"It sounded a lot sexier when he said it," Kim said. "In that Jamaican accent."

"Was he?" I asked, already knowing the answer.

She nodded. "God, yes. Huge bulge in his pants." She sounded awed.

Of course he'd been hard. She was sexy as hell. "'Huge?'" I asked.

She looked worried again.

"I won't be mad," I said. "Promise."

She nodded.

"Bigger than me?"

She nodded again. Then, "They say black guys are bigger."

"That's a myth though, right?"

"I don't know. I thought it was. But *he* was definitely bigger."

The jealousy again, stabbing through me. And

yet, at the same time, I suddenly had an image of a thick, long black cock, parting her folds. Driving up inside her. Would it stretch her? Would she like that—being stretched a little?

Academic, I told myself. I wouldn't let her go that far.

"So what now?" Kim asked.

I stopped walking and turned to look at her. Her face was lit up in the neon glow of the bar behind us and I could see her eyes shining with excitement. And also fear. Fear that this would go wrong, fear that we'd do something that would hurt us.

I slipped my arms around her waist and pulled her to me. And then I kissed her, drawing a yelp of surprise from her before it changed into an *mmm* and her lips flowered open under mine. "I love you," I said when we came up for air.

She panted and nodded, grinning. I felt as if we were unstoppable. The jealousy had burned away, leaving me with just the raw lust of seeing her dressed so sexily, the high of knowing that other men had stared, flirted, even touched...but that only I'd be going home with her.

"Do you want to head back to the hotel?" she asked. She had her palm on my chest, her touch warm through my shirt, and something in her tone told me that we'd both be tearing our clothes off as soon as we got through the hotel room door.

We should have gone back. But I wanted to play some more. The sex would be even better, afterwards, if we did it again.

"Let's do it once more," I told her.

She took a deep breath, as excited as I was. "Okay," she said. "Where?"

There was a place across the street that looked promising. Plenty of guys about our age. It had orange walls and, instead of a normal sign above the door, someone had sawed a pale blue rowing boat in half lengthwise and hung that there, with the name painted in big letters on the side: *Mulhoney's*. It looked friendly. Safe.

"There," I said. I kissed her again. "I'll be right behind you."

She hurried off into the bar. And that's when it all went wrong.

CHAPTER 7

THIS TIME, I didn't wait as long. I wanted to be there when she was approached. I wanted to see the guys look at her before moving in. I went through the door only thirty seconds or so behind Kim, but immediately turned the other way, not even looking at her, and then sidled around the room so that I could watch without being obvious.

The place was dark, dark enough that Kim's skin, in reality a light tan, gleamed almost white amongst the shadows. She threaded her way through the crowd and I marveled at the way the heels drew attention to her legs and ass. Her skirt wasn't crazy short—there were only a few inches of pale thigh visible above the knee—but, if you were to slide your hand under the tight fabric, your fingers wouldn't have far to go before they touched her panties. The thought made my cock stir...and so did the knowledge that every other guy in the place was thinking the same thing.

There was a mixture of couples and single guys in the bar, and the men all immediately perked up when they caught sight of Kim—even the ones who were there with their girlfriends. God, was *I* that obvious, when I was out with Kim and I saw a hot woman? I could actually see the wave of excitement pass through the room, radiating out from Kim as she moved. One guy moved to intercept her, but then seemed to veer off at the last moment. I frowned. What had he seen? Did he suspect she wasn't single?

Kim sat down. And just as she did so, a huge, black hand landed on her naked forearm. We both looked at the man at the same time.

It was him. The guy I'd seen from the balcony the day before. The one who'd been watching her.

I felt fear clutching at me, cold fingers of dread closing around my chest. Should I warn her? Call the whole thing off?

Why? I couldn't explain my disquiet...but there was just something about the guy. He was different to the other suitors. I realized now why the other guy had veered off—he'd seen this guy approaching. Either the dreadlocked man had some sort of reputation or he just exuded that dominant air—that if he even glanced at a woman first, she was his.

I felt sick. Not *his,* I reminded myself desperately. *Mine.* He just didn't know it, yet. He must not have noticed her ring, the previous day, or he wouldn't be making a move now. Right?

He didn't waste any time. He didn't seem to ask her what she wanted to drink, just called for the bartender to bring him a beer and some sort of cocktail for Kim. Kim looked at it warily, but accepted it and sipped as she listened to him.

He wasn't the same as the guy in the first bar. That guy had been smooth and practiced—a pick-up artist. This guy was more...raw. He didn't care about lines or following rules or making the right impression. He seemed to be just be laying it out for her, telling her what he wanted. And from his gestures and the looks he gave her...what he wanted was her.

I tried to get closer, but there was a clear gap between them and me. I'd stick out a mile if I stood in the middle. It didn't help that the guy's voice was a deep, rich baritone that got lost in the music. I could hear what Kim said, sometimes, but could only make out a word or two of what he was saying.

I realized that Kim's face had changed completely. In the previous bar, she'd appeared transfixed, as if she was hanging on every word of the guy in the orange shirt. Now, with the dreadlocked man, her face was a lot more mobile. I could actually see her nostrils flare as she breathed, and her eyes were wide and darting around his face. It looked as if her pupils were huge and dilated, and she seemed to be flushed.

She'd been acting, before. She wasn't acting now. She liked him. No, more than that. She wanted him.

Another swirl of unease inside me. I'd started this game because I wanted men to look at her. I hadn't considered that she'd start to look back at them. *You idiot! What have you started?!*

But it was okay. Kim was completely faithful. This wouldn't go any further than we both wanted it to.

But how far is that? Because, even as the electricity between them scared me, the image rose again in my head, unbidden, of the two of them together. More details, this time. His long hair tossing as he buried himself savagely in her. Her scream of passion as he thrust—

I swallowed. I didn't want that. Of course I didn't. But what if it happened anyway? What if things got out of hand? My phone was right there in my pocket. I could end it instantly....

But I didn't want to. I wanted—needed—to see more.

I was much closer than I'd been on the balcony, so I could see the guy a lot better, now. He was in smart black pants and shoes and a loose white shirt. Dressed up for a night out—perhaps for a night on the prowl. Did he already have a plan for what he was going to do with the woman he met? Did he already have it all worked out: a few drinks, then back to his place, toss her down on the bed and—

My cock was almost painfully hard inside my pants. I can't explain it, but something about the sight of them together was both terrifying and hot as hell. There was an edge to him, a danger—it felt as if we'd taken our seatbelts off.

The guy lifted one huge hand and ran it over Kim's cheek. I tensed at the intimacy of the touch—it wasn't a casual brush of the shoulder. He was full-on seducing her, right in front of me. And though she went tense at first, a second later I thought I saw her push her face against his hand just a little. I was amazed by how big his hands were—they made Kim look tiny and fragile by comparison.

I noticed he wasn't trying to get close to her. He was touching her cheek, but he wasn't trying to cozy up to her on the bar stool. He hadn't even sat down yet—he stood there hulking over her, which made him seem even bigger. He wasn't interested in just groping her, I realized. He wanted all or nothing. *He wants her in his bed.*

Again, the fear rose inside me. It was like watching a spider waiting to pounce on a fly. I'd thought I was the one in control, ready to pull my wife away when I decided the game was over. But what if I was wrong?

What if it wasn't a game at all?

Even as I thought it, the guy finished his drink and pushed back from the bar. And held out his hand towards my wife. It was almost a relief. It was over—there was no way she was going to go with him.

Then she took his hand.

My jaw fell open. I watched as Kim slid off her bar stool and hurried after him, letting him tow her through the crowd. She didn't even glance back at me.

Maybe he wanted to dance. Maybe that was it. Maybe they were just going to—

They walked out through the door and onto the street.

My eyes bugged out and I froze there for long, agonizing seconds. What the hell was going on? Why would she go with him? That wasn't part of the plan! When I was finally able to move again, I raced for the door and burst out onto the street, stopping in the center.

They were nowhere in sight.

I looked frantically up and down the street, searching the crowds for them. Nothing. I spun in a slow circle. My heart was hammering in my chest, dread panic setting in. I'd lost her. She was in some back alley, or in the back of a cab, or—

Just as I completed the circle, I saw her. She'd been almost directly behind me, still hand-in-hand with the dreadlocked man. They were just disappearing into the bar next to the one they'd been in. I'd run right past them.

Weak with relief, I hurried after them.

This bar was more ramshackle, furnished with a real mixture of old furniture and tables made from what looked like driftwood. Towards the back of the room, it got pretty dark. As I watched him lead her along, it hit me just how much bigger he was. I'd been right—even in her high heels, he was a full head taller than Kim and a good bit taller than me. And his broad shoulders made him seem twice her width, even though he was tight and lean with muscle. If someone had told me he was a linebacker with some NFL team, I wouldn't have argued.

As I followed them, I saw there were booths there, each one seating four, or six if you were very friendly. I saw him direct her into one of the booths, both sitting on the same long seat.

No! Don't go in there! I won't be able to—

But it was too late. They were sitting down, and now they were private—which I was sure was what he wanted. I couldn't stand there and watch them, not without looking obvious.

Maybe I shouldn't care about that, anymore. Maybe I should just march up to the guy and tell him Kim was my wife, and that I was taking her home now.

But...now that the adrenaline was soaking out of me, some of the arousal was coming back. He'd spirited her out of one bar, only to take her here. And he'd made sure they were somewhere private. Why? What was he planning?

I only had seconds to decide. I was still walking and, once I reached their booth, I couldn't just hang around beside it—

Making a snap decision, I slid myself into the booth across the room from theirs. I sat on the opposite side, so that I was facing them diagonally. Now I could see them, though I'd have to make sure I didn't ogle them too openly. I realized that the booths were made from old church pews, their dark wood adding to the moody gloom of the place.

The dreadlocked man had made sure that Kim

went into the booth first, so his massive body was blocking her from leaving. Not that she showed any signs of wanting to leave. She still had that look of breathless excitement on her face. I wasn't sure I'd ever seen that exact look before. It was almost as if she was drugged—had he slipped something in her drink? But it had started almost the instant they'd met, before she'd even sipped her cocktail.

Did she like him—want him—that much? Was that it? A pang of jealousy stabbed deep in my chest, but mostly what I felt was shock. I hadn't really thought of Kim having strong desires like that—certainly not for other men. She'd always been a very controlled person. The idea that she could lust after someone so much that she'd take chances, like walking off with a stranger, was a revelation...and a turn on.

A waiter came around to ask them what they wanted, only to greet the dreadlocked man with delighted surprise. And that's how I finally learned the name of the man who was seducing my wife: Jaric. The waiter and Jaric did a complicated handshake and Jaric introduced my wife as "Kim." The sight of him introducing his date to his buddy did something weird to me. It felt *wrong*. To them, my wife was just another single white tourist, probably the latest in a long line of Jaric's conquests. He might as well have told his friend, "This is the one I'm fucking tonight." It made me feel helpless, even though I was sitting right there across the room. Helpless...and turned on. Wasn't this exactly what I'd wanted? My wife lusted after and discussed as an object of desire?

The waiter came over to me to ask what I wanted. I started to order a beer, but then realized that the waiter wasn't listening—he was looking back over his shoulder toward Jaric and my wife. I paused, and when the waiter realized he'd been caught, he snapped back to face me. "Sorry," he said, abashed. Then, nodding his head toward Jaric and my wife and grinning, "Lucky man."

I sat there stunned, not knowing whether to fume or smile. *She's mine,* I wanted to say. But I just ordered my beer and sat back.

Jaric had his hand in my wife's hair, now, the golden strands falling between his thick fingers as he brushed it back from her face. She was breathing faster—I could see that gorgeous tan cleavage rising and falling, and I swore she was almost trembling with excitement.

And right then, just for a second, she glanced across and saw me. And to my surprise, her eyes widened in shock, she gave a quick smile, and then her eyes were back on him again.

She hadn't known I was there.

I'd been assuming that she'd been watching out for me, making sure I was still with her. But she'd been so lost in the adventure that she hadn't even seen me take my seat. I was suddenly angry with her. What if I hadn't seen her going into the bar? What if I'd been held up?

Calm down, I told myself. *You started this.*

The waiter returned with our drinks—a beer for Jaric and me and another cocktail for my wife. She'd be tipsy after this one, I estimated, but not drunk.

Almost as soon as the waiter was gone, Jaric made his move. With one foot, he pushed the driftwood table back from the pew, opening up some space. Then he slid a muscled arm around my wife's waist and lifted her onto his lap.

Just before she landed, the dim lights of the bar caught the fabric of Jaric's pants and, for the first time, I could see the bulge there. It was huge, extending well down his thigh. And when Kim's soft rump touched down on top of it, her widening eyes told me that she could feel it, too.

I looked away. I didn't want to, but I knew that if I kept staring at them, Jaric was going to notice and suspect something. I couldn't bear not seeing what was going on, though. I was just too far away to hear exactly what they were saying, but I could make out the tone of their voices. I could hear murmured conversation, a soft, nervous giggle from my wife and the low, rumbling voice of Jaric. They talked for long minutes, and I heard the sounds my wife was making change. The nervous giggles died away, and her responses to his questions became lower and slower. Her voice trembling with...arousal?

I made out something that sounded like *feel good,* but the combination of his low tone and the patois made it difficult to be sure. Then I heard *real good.*

I had an idea. I put my phone on the table, leaning it on its side propped up against my beer bottle, with the camera lens in the back pointed roughly towards Jaric and Kim's booth. I started the video camera app, and suddenly I could see, on the tiny screen, what was happening across the room.

Kim was still sitting on Jaric's lap, but now he had one meaty forearm across her waist, holding her in place. Her head was back against his massive shoulder, her blonde hair trailing down his arm. With one hand, he was rubbing her bare midriff, slowly and tenderly. His other hand was on her knee.

And it was sliding higher, rubbing as it went.

My wife squirmed, but it wasn't a *stop* squirm. It was an *I like what you're doing to me* squirm. It was dark in the bar and even darker in the shadows under the table, but there was enough light that I could clearly see Jaric's dark hand against my wife's skin, moving higher and higher. His fingertips nudged the hem of her skirt.

Okay, I thought. *That's it. That's where she'll stop him.*

But the hand went higher, until his fingers were on her bare thigh, rubbing back and forth. I saw Kim draw in a slow breath and her lips parted, but she didn't say anything. It was as if she was hypnotized. And then her thighs inched ever so slightly apart.

He's touching my wife! He's got his hand up her skirt! The rational part of my brain was screaming at me, demanding that I stop this. But with every inch that Jaric's fingers moved, my cock grew harder. How far would she let it go, if I didn't stop her?

Jaric started to murmur something, speaking almost into Kim's ear, and again she squirmed. Whatever he was saying seemed to be turning her on. Her breathing quickened, her skin almost glowing with her heated arousal. The hand slid further up under her skirt. And then still further. I gasped. *God, he must be touching her—*

Kim drew in her breath, her eyes widening. I saw her lips press together into a soft line and she started to move ever so slightly on his lap, in time with his hand. He was rubbing her. Rubbing her pussy lips through her panties. I could imagine the soft warmth of her through the thin fabric. *The bastard's feeling her up, right in front of me!*

The hand started to move faster. I saw Jaric's wrist flex as he pressed his fingers more firmly against her. And his other hand was moving, now sliding up to her chest. I gasped as I saw him cup her breast through her shirt. *They've only just met! How can he— How could she—*

Kim seemed uncertain for a second. I saw her swallow. She glanced down at her chest, then up at him. But her eyes were shining and bright and, when he moved his head in towards hers, she closed her eyes and parted her lips.

He's—Wait, is he going to—

He kissed her. Soft and then harder, and she kissed him back just as hard. Their heads moved together in a dance, falling into it as easily as lovers.

We'd never talked about kissing. I sat there stunned, staring at the screen. His tongue was deep in her mouth, plundering my wife, *violating* her...and she wanted it. I wasn't ready for how it made me feel, somehow much worse than the hand on her breast or the fingers on her pussy.

And yet I didn't want it to stop. Every second I sat there, I felt my cock straining harder and harder in my pants, even as the rage built inside me.

His hand was moving on her breast. Squeezing the soft flesh, making it bulge between his fingers. My wife gave an audible groan through the kiss. The hand under her skirt was moving faster now, his fingers circling as they rubbed. My wife was moving, too, grinding against the hand, squirming in his lap and circling her hips.

I thought I saw him smile, as he kissed her.

Then his hand was pushing the purple shirt aside and cupping her breast through her bra. She'd worn a simple white one, since the edge of it would show around the shirt, and it was thin enough that, as he moved his hand, I could detect the outline of her nipple through the fabric. But that wasn't enough for him. He obviously wanted to feel her breast naked against his hand, and the bra cup was too tight.

So he simply grabbed hold of the cup and yanked on it until it ripped, the stitching coming loose where it joined the strap. Then he was able to easily push it down, and suddenly my wife's naked breast was exposed.

I almost stood up in my seat. I saw Kim break away from the kiss for a second, alerted by the feel and sound of the garment ripping, but then his palm pressed to her naked breast and she just moaned into his mouth. The kiss resumed, and now he was rolling her breast in his hand, his thumb stroking over the nipple again and again. I could see the pink nub stiff and erect each time his thumb moved away. I couldn't believe what I was seeing. It held me frozen.

The fingers on her pussy had never stopped moving. They were moving faster and faster, and I could see the flush rising in her cheeks—

Jesus, he was going to—

She was panting into his mouth, her hands coming up to clutch at the muscles of his arms—

The realization shook me out of my stupor. I stood up, turning towards their booth, and suddenly I was seeing in person what I'd only been witnessing on my phone's screen.

Kim sat atop Jaric, her legs squeezed together around Jaric's massive forearm. Her back was pressed to his chest, one huge black hand fondling her breast. They were still kissing deep and fast, but I could see her panting and moaning through the kiss—

Stop!

Too late.

Kim lifted her lips from Jaric's no more than a few millimeters and let out a long, sharp cry, loud enough to be heard by me—and half the bar. A rising, keening moan that left no doubt as to what was happening. I saw Jaric's fingers rub even faster, and at her breast I saw his thumb and forefinger take her nipple and gently squeeze.

She bucked atop him, arching her back, every muscle going rigid. Her fingers scrabbled and clawed at his arms and this time I was sure I saw him smile. Kim trembled, twitched...and went still.

She was facing towards me. When she opened her eyes, the first thing she saw was my horrified face.

I quickly walked away, my head spinning. I burst out of the door of the bar and into the open air, then staggered to a stop. The blood was pounding in my ears, shock and betrayal pushing thorns deep into my heart.

Victoria Kasari

CHAPTER 8

A MOMENT LATER, Kim stumbled out, her eyes wide and her hair mussed. She'd pulled her shirt and bra up to cover herself, but her face was still flushed. I recognized that glow from when we'd have sex.

She came. She had an orgasm with another man.

She grabbed my arm. I started walking.

"Lewis, what—Is it okay? Are we okay?" she asked desperately.

I couldn't answer. I didn't know how I felt. I just shook my head and led the way back to the hotel. We didn't speak until we got inside our room. Even then, I didn't say anything immediately. I just paced silently, trying to control my rage. I wanted to kill Jaric. A part of me wanted to kill Kim, too.

"Isn't that what you wanted?" she asked at last.

"No!" I said automatically. "You were just meant to flirt and—and—"

"We said touching was okay!"

"*Touching,* but that wasn't—Jesus, Kim, he made you come!"

She looked at the floor. "It wasn't—I didn't know it was going to—"

"You could have stopped him! Or did he have his tongue too far down your throat?"

Her face blossomed red. "*You* could have stopped it! You didn't call!"

I opened my mouth to shout at her, but stopped short.

"Why didn't you?" she demanded.

I didn't have an answer.

"Because you were enjoying it?" she asked, in a tone that suggested she already knew the answer.

I blustered, my hands squeezing into fists, but I couldn't deny it. I had been enjoying it. Right up until it went too far—

No. That wasn't true. If I was truthful, I'd enjoyed it even then. Watching her come had been a brutal, visceral shock, but the memory of it, still fresh in my mind, made me immediately hard.

"You liked it, didn't you?" she said savagely.

I finally nodded.

"Then don't get mad at me!" she snapped.

I looked her in the eyes and realized for the first time that she was close to crying. Immediately, I felt sick. I'd started this whole game. I'd brought us out to Jamaica to try to respark things and, instead, I'd driven us apart. "Sorry," I said, pulling her to me. "I'm sorry."

She pressed herself against me and sniffed, but I'd caught her just in time: the tears didn't actually come out. "I'm sorry too," she said. "I went too far."

I shook my head. "It was my fault. We should have made sure we were clear about what we wanted. And..."—I sighed—"I'm not sure it's even what you did. It was that I didn't expect it."

"Did it feel like I was cheating on you?" she asked in a quiet voice.

"Yeah. A little."

She looked at the floor. I put my hand under her chin and tilted her face up to look at me, but she wouldn't meet my eyes. "But if I had to do it again, and we talked about it first, and you asked me if it was okay if that happened..." I bit my lip and shook my head as I thought about it. "I think I'd say 'yes'."

When I said that, she finally looked me in the eye. "Really?"

"Really."

"You liked watching me come with another man?"

Hearing her say it was a shock—almost a slap in the face. And yet, even as the words blazed in my brain, they seemed to soak straight into my body and throb down to my cock. "Yes," I said tightly.

I looked at her, then. I took in what he'd done to her. Her hair was mussed, where he'd run his fingers through it again and again. Her lipstick was smeared where his mouth had pressed hungrily to hers. Her bra was ripped, the cup hanging limply from its strap. "Lift your skirt," I ordered, my voice thick with lust.

She inched it up her thighs. Her panties were dark green. And right at the front, there was a darker green patch where the moisture had soaked through the fabric.

My wife, with all the traces of a man having enjoyed her. Used her.

She'd never looked sexier.

"You're wet," I said. "Christ, you're really wet."

"Soaking. I've never...not so fast. Not like that."

I stood there staring at her. I couldn't take my eyes off that patch of moisture. And I felt all the anger drain from me. I wasn't angry at her...I wasn't even angry at Jaric. Hell, he didn't even know she was married. All he'd done was play his part. If anyone was at fault, it was me. And as the anger went, what was left behind was raw, scorching lust.

She stepped close to me, close enough that I could feel her breath on my chest. "Are we okay, then?" she asked.

I nodded, slowly and solemnly so that she'd know I was telling the truth. "I'm sorry," I said. "I freaked out. Can we just rewind?"

"You mean, pretend tonight never happened?"

I shook my head. "No. I want it to have happened." I met her eyes and we looked at one another for a long moment. Eventually, we both allowed tentative smiles to creep onto our faces.

"What do you want to do, then?" she asked.

"The jacuzzi," I said. "Let's go out there."

When I'd booked, caught up in the enthusiasm, I'd sprung for one of the luxury suites. One of the perks was a balcony with a view of the ocean...and a jacuzzi. Our room was up on the fifth floor and the balcony wasn't overlooked.

"In swimsuits?" she asked tentatively.

"No. Not in swimsuits." And I pulled off my shirt. My eyes locked again on her groin.

She smiled again, and this time it grew into a full-on grin. She undid the purple shirt and took it off. With it gone, I could really see her ripped bra, and the sight of it sent a wave of heat through me. God, the guy had been an animal.

She tossed the bra in the trash and stood there topless, her full breasts bouncing as she straightened up. Her nipples, I noticed, were standing erect again. She unzipped the skirt and let it fall around her feet, and pulled off her heels. And then it was just the green panties.

She slowly slid them down her hips. I could see

her waxed pussy lips puffy and swollen, still shining with slickness. I'd seen the same sight many times before, but it had always been me who had brought her to that state, my body she'd hungered for.

I stepped closer and cupped her gently, my fingers against her pussy, the back of my hand brushing her still-warm panties as they lay stretched around her thighs. Looking into her eyes, I pushed a finger into her. God, she was soaking and hot. Hot for him. There was a caveman part of me that wanted to slap her. Another, much stronger part of me, wanted to kiss her as hard as I could.

So I did. I mashed my lips down on hers and immediately she opened to me. A moan escaped her: relief, maybe, and joy. My tongue plunged into her mouth and it was as if I was reclaiming what was mine. My hand slid into the hair at the back of her head and I held her there, and she didn't protest. In fact, she pushed herself against me, her naked breasts squashing against my bare chest.

When we finally broke for air, I almost wanted to forget the jacuzzi and just pull her onto the bed. But I drew my finger from her, her moisture shining there, and quickly slipped off the rest of my clothes. Then I led her out onto the balcony.

She was hesitant at first, until she'd reassured herself that we weren't overlooked. But as soon as her feet hit the steaming water, she relaxed. She gave a growl of pleasure, closely followed by one from me, as we slid in right up to our necks.

We stared at each other across the water. I hadn't hit the button to start the bubbles, so the surface was calm, with little twists of steam rising up between us. The heat soaked all the tension out of my body.

"Sorry," I said again.

She nodded. I looked down through the water

at her smooth, tan body, her breasts bobbing and bouncing under the surface, the small patch of blonde hair between her legs gleaming.

"You look incredible," I told her. Then, "You know when the waiter came over? He said Jaric was a lucky guy."

She flushed. It was amazing to me that, after everything she'd done that evening, it was a compliment that was most able to make her redden. "He really said that?" she asked, delighted.

I nodded. "And he was right."

She looked down at the water, embarrassed. But when she met my eyes again, she was grinning.

"What was he like?" I asked.

"You know what he was like," she said. "You were right there."

"I didn't mean physically. I meant what he's like—how he...seduced you. But actually...yeah, tell me what you like about him. Physically."

She raised an eyebrow. "You sure?"

I nodded.

"Well...he's *big*. I mean, obviously he's big."

"You like that?" I broke in. "I didn't know you went for...'big.' And muscles."

"Neither did I," she told me. "I mean, I guess I did. I see guys on calendars, and at the gym, but those guys look kind of...plastic. Jaric's not plastic. He's just big, like he's made like that, you know? Like men say they like real breasts over fake breasts. He feels real, you know?"

I nodded.

"And he's not just tall. He's wide. He makes me feel small."

I remembered how she'd looked, being led by the hand. Fragile.

"His hands are really big." She swallowed, remembering. "And warm. Dry, but warm. And he

84

smells really good. I don't know what it is, something that smells like spices or incense. Not weed. Something else. And he's *hella* good looking."

I blinked at that. "Really? I mean, you know, I guessed he was, but I'm not a good judge. You go for...black men?"

She thought about it. "I go for this one. Hell yeah. He's got those soulful eyes, chocolate brown. *Dark.* And he sort of broods. Good jaw. And I like the dreads, too. They work on him. They look all wild."

None of that made sense to me. What the hell were "soulful eyes?" I guessed it was a woman thing. But all that mattered was that she thought he was hot. I thought about the bulge I'd seen. "And when you were sitting on him...."

But she didn't take the hint. "Yeah, when I was sitting on him, his thighs felt *solid.* Like tree trunks, or something. And his arms, when he wrapped one around me—just really big and heavy. I felt as if I could swing from them or anything, and he wouldn't flinch. And they made me feel...I don't know. Protected."

"I meant...*between* his legs."

"Oh!" She giggled and I smiled. "Yeah. That." She flushed again.

"Be honest. Was he big?"

"You mean, bigger than you?"

Now it was my turn to flush. It felt weird—hotly humiliating and yet a turn on at the same time. I can't explain it. "Yeah. Was he bigger than me?"

She nodded slowly, watching my reaction. "Yeah. I mean, a lot bigger. Not that you're small. But yes. A lot."

I'd like to say I took it well, but I went quiet and stared off into the distance.

"I mean, it was probably *too* big," said Kim quickly. "I'm not sure I'd even want one that big."

I looked at her. "Liar," I said tenderly.

She lowered her eyes. I was discovering more and more new things about my wife.

"Maybe I would," she said at last. "But I don't know."

I said nothing. I just looked at her. In my head, I had that image again, of a huge, black cock parting the soft pink lips of her sex.

There was a long pause. She took in my silence, my expression. She looked down through the water between us and saw my cock standing hard.

"You'd like it?" she asked. Her voice was low and had an edge of lust to it. "You'd like to see me take a big cock?"

I nodded.

"You'd like to see me take a big...*black* cock?" she asked.

I stared right at her and nodded again. Then, "I mean, the *idea* of it. Not actually do it. I wouldn't want it to go any further than we already have."

Kim nodded quickly. "Maybe we could get a toy, or something. Like a dildo."

I thought about that. The two of us in bed together, and her opening her thighs for a huge rubber cock. It sounded hot...although not as hot as the images in my head. "Maybe," I said. "Can you tell me about him? Not his body, but what he said? How did he get you so..." I searched for the right words. "I mean, five or ten minutes, and he'd persuaded you to leave with him. Another ten or fifteen and you were in his lap, coming your brains out."

She leaned back against the edge of the jacuzzi. That made her breasts rise to the surface, the nipples just breaking through the water, which made it hard for me to think. "He was aggressive," she said slowly, remembering. "Not bad-aggressive. Good-aggressive."

I scrunched up my brow. "There's a good-aggressive?"

She nodded. "Like...he knew exactly what he wanted. He was very confident. There was no watching me across the room, waiting for the right moment. He just walked right up to me and put a hand on me and ordered me a drink, and then told me—not asked, told me—that I should have some fun with him."

"He sounds like an asshole," I said.

"It wasn't like that. He's just very cool and confident and there's a bit of humor, too, and...he makes you kind of want to go along with whatever he says. Because if you don't you feel like you're missing out. Plus, he sort of orders you."

"He really does sound like an asshole."

"I know, but I'm not explaining it well. He's sort of...dominant."

"Dominant? Like leather pants and whip dominant?"

"No. Yes. I don't know. Maybe. Alpha male-y. Like you don't argue with him. You just don't."

I remembered the feeling I'd got, when I'd first seen him watching Kim. That sense that he wasn't like the others. I'd been right, but it didn't make me feel any better. "He'd seen you before," I told her. "He was watching you, last night. When you were sitting at the table on your own. He was there watching you."

I thought that would disturb her. In fact, I think that was my aim, in telling her. But it had the opposite effect. "He was?!" she asked, excitedly.

Jaric almost seemed to have cast a spell on her. He'd talked to her for less than a half hour, total, and she seemed as smitten with him as a teenage girl crushing on a rock star. "You know you scared the hell out of me," I said, "when you left the bar with him."

She shrugged. "He said he was taking me to the bar next door. That's where he works. He's a barman."

"And you just trusted him?" I was trying not to get angry, but the *alpha male* thing had rubbed me up the wrong way. Mainly, I think, because I had a horrible suspicion that whatever this alpha male thing was, this elusive X-factor that Kim liked so much, it was something I didn't possess. "What if he'd abducted you, or something?"

"I knew you'd be right behind me. You were, right?"

"I was. Not that you noticed. You just went straight into the next place with him. I almost lost you!" I was snapping at her, now.

She stiffened and stood up. Her naked breasts lifted completely clear of the water, her skin shining wetly. "I *did* notice. I stopped and held back, before we went into the next bar. I waited until you came out. I saw you blunder out of the bar and look around, all panicked, and I waited until you saw us before I went into the next one."

I blinked. She hadn't even looked at me—

"I was looking at your reflection in the window," she told me patiently.

Oh. All my anger slipped away. "Sorry," I said humbly.

She sighed. "It's okay. You were only worried about me. And I *did* lose sight of you for a while inside, until we were sitting down in the booths." She paused. "That isn't what you were annoyed about, though, is it?"

I tried to ignore the question, but she just stood

there staring at me until I folded. "Is he really different to me?" I asked. "This whole dominant alpha male thing? Is that not...me? I mean, does he do something for you I can't?" It all came out in a rush.

"Oh, honey!" she rushed forward, water sloshing around her waist. I stood up and she flung her arms around me. "Honey, I love you! He's not *competing* against you! He's just...different."

"Better?" I pressed.

"Different." She sighed and stepped back, so she could look at me. She ran a hand through her hair, wetting it. "It's like...damn it, I can't think of an analogy. It's like...sometimes, you think it'd be fun to drive...a Lamborghini, right? All raw power and crazy fast. But you wouldn't want that every day. It'd drive you nuts."

"So what am *I?*" I asked, aghast.

"You're like the car I *can* drive every day. You make me happy."

"I'm a *Toyota?!* What, I'm a fucking Prius?"

"No, no! You're like...a BMW or something, okay? I can live with you, every day but you're still fun and exciting and everyone wants you."

I went quiet. "Fun and exciting?" I said after a while.

"Yes!"

"Everyone wants me?"

"If it makes you feel better, Jenny definitely thinks you're hot. We've joked about it." Jenny was one of her married friends. It did actually make me feel a little better.

"So I'm a BMW," I said. Then my voice sank. "But not a Lamborghini."

"But I don't want a Lamborghini," Kim said, exasperated. "A Lamborghini would drive me crazy. It's totally unsuitable for me. I'm not sure I could control it. And I'm not sure I could handle that much...power."

I met her eyes. "But you like to fantasize about it?"

She nodded.

"And maybe you'd like to drive one...just once?"

She hesitated...then nodded again. I understood, then. I wasn't happy, but I got it. And the more I thought about her and Jaric, the more turned on I got. After all, we were never going to see the guy again. Now that it was over, the whole experience was just fantasy material. Very good fantasy material.

I put my hands on her waist. My cock was rising stiffly up to stand like an iron rod between us. We both glanced down at it. Then I pushed her back and motioned for her to sit on the edge of the jacuzzi. She did it, a slow smile spreading across her face. I ran my hands over her wet shoulders and then down to her breasts, weighing them in my hands.

"That's it," she said, grinning. "Forget him. That's all over. It's just us, now."

I lifted her breasts, running my thumbs over her nipples, the way he'd done. "No."

"No?"

"No." I sank to my knees in the jacuzzi. That put my head just a little above the water... and right on a level with Kim's groin. "Tell me." I pressed her thighs apart with my shoulders.

Her eyes widened. "Tell you what?" she squeaked.

"Tell me about what he did to you," I said, my voice almost a growl. As I opened her thighs wider, her outer lips parted. The water might have washed away the slickness, but I knew that inside, she was still hotly wet for him. I pushed forward, my lips brushing her soft folds.

"Ah! O—Okay. He told me to sit on him. And I didn't want to do it at first because I was embarrassed, but his voice just made me go all gooey and soft inside, so I...I sat down on him...."

I plunged my tongue between her lips. Immediately, I could taste the sweet musk of her, the wetness of her arousal. I slid my hands from her breasts and put one on each of her thighs, keeping them braced apart. Then I started to lick, my tongue questing into her folds.

"God! He wrapped an arm around me to hold me there. I was trapped, in a way, but...it felt good. And he rubbed my stomach. I don't know why. No one's ever done that, before. And then his hand was going up my leg—"

I moved my hand higher up her thigh, lifting my face from her, bringing my fingers to her pussy lips. "Like this?"

"Ah! Yes, like that. Rubbing. Rubbing me...and I wasn't sure if we should, because you were right there, but you didn't tell me to stop. And I could— Ah!—I could feel myself getting hot, and wet, I could feel my panties getting wet as he rubbed, and his fingers were so big, so strong. He pushed so hard they went inside me, a little, even with my panties on. And I wanted it."

"You wanted his fingers inside you?" My voice was low and hoarse.

"Yes! I wanted his fingers inside me. Right up inside me. I wanted him to pull my panties to one side and shove them up inside me, but he didn't. He just kept rubbing, faster and faster, and then he undid my shirt and grabbed my breast—"

I palmed one breast and squeezed. "Like this?"

"Y—Yes—Harder! Yes! And I felt him rip my

bra and he was rubbing and rubbing, and we were kissing, and I knew I was going to come in front of you, in front of my husband, and I wasn't wearing my ring—"

I stood up, pushed her legs even wider and rammed my cock into her sopping folds in one movement. She gave a moan of need like I'd never heard before and her hands closed on my naked ass, pulling me in even harder. I was hilted in her, feeling the heat of her around me. "This is what you wanted, isn't it?" I snapped. I was angry and horny and out of control. I started to thrust. "You wanted to be fucked, didn't you?"

"Yes!" she gasped.

"You wanted to be fucked like this, didn't you?" God, she was so hot and tight around me, a clutching, silken tunnel.

"Yes!"

"Only you didn't want my cock, did you? You wanted a big black cock, didn't you?"

"Don't—"

I grabbed her hips, the smooth flesh slippery under my fingers. "You wanted Jaric's cock, didn't you?"

"No—I—"

But her pussy had clenched around me the instant I said his name. "You did, didn't you? Tell me!"

"Yes," she gasped. She was pressing herself hard against me, her breasts pillowing against my chest, her nipples hard as rocks.

I was fucking him out of her. That's how it felt, to my caveman brain. I was taking back my property. "You wanted him, didn't you, you slut!"

"*Yes!*" And suddenly she was coming, bucking and shuddering around me, her fingers digging hard into my ass, and I was thrusting harder and faster than I ever had before, knowing that in a second, I was going to—

"Pull out!" she said breathlessly. "God, pull out! You're not wearing a condom!"

For another few seconds, I kept thrusting.

"Pull out!" she insisted. And this time, I pulled out of her. Just in time for my cock to erupt, long ropes of cum shooting across her stomach and the underside of her breasts. We both watched it happen, panting. And then I sat down heavily on the edge of the jacuzzi next to her, and we just stared at each other.

"God," she said. "It's never been like *that* before."

I nodded. Then laughed. I couldn't help it. I felt incredible.

"It was close," I said when I'd stopped. "Do you think we...I mean, do you think it's okay?"

She looked down at the lines of cum criss-crossing her body. "Given how much you managed to shoot on me, I can't believe any went off early. I think we're okay. It's way too risky to be a regular thing, though. Back to condoms for you, mister, until we're ready."

I nodded, a little sad. Being inside her, without a condom for once, had felt incredible. But she was right—we weren't ready to start a family quite yet. I could wait until the fall. It was only a matter of months.

"Was it good?" she asked.

I nodded, the grin almost splitting my face apart. "Hell yeah. You?"

She nodded. Then, "You know you called me a slut."

I blinked. "Did I?"

She nodded, giving me a look.

Now I thought about it, I did remember

snarling something along those lines at one point. "God! Sorry."

She blushed, but smirked. "It's okay. I kind of feel like a slut."

We lapsed into silence for a second.

"What happens now?" she asked. "I mean, do you think you want to play that game again— showing me off? Or is it over? Or what?"

I thought about it. It had been scary as hell at a few points. And we'd very nearly had a huge row. But we'd also had hands-down the best sex we'd had in a long time.

"Let's sleep on it," I said.

CHAPTER 9

WHEN I OPENED MY EYES the next morning, I'd had a really weird dream. I'd taken my wife to some bar and stood there and watched while a stranger—

I sat up and looked around. We really were in Jamaica. Our clothes were still strewn around the floor from the night before, including Kim's green panties. It wasn't a dream.

***

We hit the beach for the first time. The fresh air and gleaming white sand made the dark bars of the night before seem a million miles away. Kim wore the metallic red swimsuit I'd bought her and, out in the daylight, she looked even more stunning in it than she had in the store. It clung to every inch of her bountiful chest and the high-cut legs made her long thighs seem even longer.

We lay there basking in the heat, side by side, and the silence and stillness gave me a chance to try to work out what was going on in my head. It felt as if we'd been through the emotional wringer, but I was pretty sure we were better for it, as a couple. Certainly, the sex had been better than it had in a long time. And we both had a head full of fantasy material to take home with us. Maybe we could do as she'd suggested, and get a toy that could take the place of Jaric's big, black cock. Or maybe—

No. We weren't doing it again. We'd gotten away with it twice: once with Thomas—the guy in the orange shirt—and then, much more extreme, with Jaric. I wasn't going to risk it again, however horny it made me. We'd done what I'd wanted— we'd found the spark or relit the fire or put the spice back or whatever the hell you wanted to call it. Now we could enjoy a great holiday and go home happy.

There was another reason I was ready to call an end to it, too. I'd discovered a lot about myself in the previous forty-eight hours. I'd discovered I liked men looking at my wife—to the extent that I'd sit passively by and watch her be gawked at. I'd discovered I liked watching her being seduced...touched. And I even liked—as a fantasy— the idea of another man fucking her. Especially a black man.

What if things kept going further and further? What if we got to the stage where some guy was ready to fuck her, and she asked me if it was okay? It wasn't that I thought I'd say "no" and she'd go ahead anyway. It was that I was scared I might say "yes." What would that mean? What sort of man would that make me?

No. No way. Safer to stop now, while we were ahead. I stopped short of saying it to Kim, though. I figured it was something we should discuss back in our room, maybe over a glass of wine. Especially because the conversation would probably lead to sex.

Towards noon, I was sitting on the towel with Kim between my legs. She was leaning forward, her hair brushed down over one shoulder and out of the way while I rubbed sunblock into her back. It was a serene, loving moment. I can't remember ever feeling so relaxed.

A shadow fell over us. I ignored it at first, figuring it was someone stopping for a moment as they strolled along the beach. But when I looked up, a pair of black feet in sandals were pointing right at Kim, only a few feet away.

I looked up. The sun was backlighting the guy, making it difficult to see him. But, as I squinted, his face came into view, grinning down at my wife.

Jaric.

"Well now." It was the first time I'd heard his voice up close. It was as rich and dark as the local coffee, warm with spice and danger, and so deep it seemed to vibrate through you. Kim's head snapped up and she stared straight into his eyes. "I didn't expect that. You tell me you're flying home the next morning, and you run off. But now you're on the beach. And married."

Kim's head snapped up and she stared right into his eyes. Her wedding ring gleamed in the sunlight. It seemed stupid to try to deny it.

"I—" I swallowed, feeling like a kid who'd been caught with his hand in the cookie jar. My brain refused to work. Jaric was part of our fantasies. We'd left him safely behind in his bar. He wasn't meant to be out here in the real world, in the daylight!

He probably thinks she was having an affair, I realized. "I knew all about it," I said quickly. It seemed important to take control, or try to. I didn't want to look like an idiot who didn't know what his wife was doing. "We were...." I looked at Kim for help, but she was just sitting there frozen, her face pale. "Um."

Jaric squatted down on his heels. God, he was so *big!* He was in board shorts and a t-shirt, his muscled thighs looking as big around as Kim's waist. He just looked at us expectantly, still grinning.

"We're sorry," I said at last. "We were, um...playing a game."

Jaric grinned even wider. "Don't be sorry. You think you're the first people to come to Jamaica and tease the men?"

I opened and closed my mouth a few times. "We didn't—I mean, we didn't mean to tease—" Knowing full well that was exactly what we'd been doing.

"You were there in my bar, while this sweet thing was sitting on my knee," Jaric said. "I recognize you."

"Yes," I admitted.

"You got a name, mon?"

I swallowed. "Lewis."

"You like what you see, Lewis? You like the way this sweet thing shakes about, when my fingers are rubbin' on the doors o' heaven?"

I could barely breathe. The last thing I'd expected was to be confronted by the third side of our little triangle. It was meant to be a game. I—we—were meant to have all the power, teasing Jaric and then pulling Kim away just in time. It wasn't meant to be like this!

I suddenly understood what Kim had been trying to say about Jaric—he *did* have a commanding tone, like you'd be an idiot to even try arguing with it. "I—Yes," I said at last.

Jaric sat down fully on the towel, without being

asked. That put him only inches away from Kim, who hadn't spoken since he arrived. "Hello, Kim," he said teasingly.

Kim was blushing, now. She couldn't look him in the eye.

"You're lookin' good. I like the red on you. That your idea, Lewis? You buy her this?" And as he said it, he leaned forward and ran one huge, black finger over the thin shoulder strap. He wasn't touching *her*, exactly, just the material. But she still drew in her breath.

"Yes," I croaked.

"It's good. She looks all science fiction. Like the queen of Mars, ready to rule." He threw back his head and laughed, shaking out his dreads. The beach was busy, by then, but his rich, booming laugh still turned heads. I felt myself flush. This section of the beach was packed with white tourists from the hotels—for once, Jaric was the one who stood out. Would people wonder who he was? Would they guess that we and he were.... *What? In a threesome? That he was Kim's sort-of lover?*

"So what do you want to do?" Jaric said in his low rumble. As simple as that. Seven words. But they changed everything because, for the first time, it was obvious that he wanted things to continue.

He knew Kim was married. He knew we'd been playing a game with him. And he didn't care.

"I—" I tried to find the words. "I don't—I mean, I think we're—"

Jaric suddenly laid his huge hand on Kim's bare thigh. She caught her breath. Both of us stared at it, black skin on light tan.

"I'll tell you what I'm thinkin'," Jaric said. "You both come with me, back to my bar. It's quiet now. I'm not workin'. We up upstairs, to my little place. And we see what happens."

My heart was thumping in my chest. Was he seriously suggesting—Right in front of me?! My head snapped around to stare at Kim.

She was gazing back at him, open-mouthed. But her eyes had that look in them again, the same one I'd seen the night before. Almost hypnotized.

I noticed something else. Her nipples had risen to attention, making raised bumps in the smooth metallic swimsuit. I glanced at Jaric and he'd noticed it, too.

"What do you think, Kim?" he asked. "You want to have some more fun? Lewis will be in the front row, this time."

Kim just stared back at him, face flushed, eyes shining. Then, at last, she shook her head.

"Alright. No problem. I'll be in my bar"—he smirked—"if you change your mind."

He stood up, throwing us into his massive shadow again, and walked off. The ground almost seemed to shake under his feet.

We sat there in shocked silence.

"*God,*" whispered Kim.

I just sat there watching his retreating back. When I lost sight of him, I turned to her. "You didn't want to?" I looked at her nipples, still hard. "You *did* want to...didn't you?"

Kim looked fearful, then stared down at her feet.

I made my voice gentler. "It's okay," I said. "But...you did want to?"

She nodded.

My stomach lurched. Sex with him as a fantasy was one thing, but this was different. Horribly real. "I—I'm not sure—"

She twisted around on the towel to look at me. "God...I'm not saying we should do it!"

We stared at each other again.

"I just mean...I mean, you asked, so I'm being honest," she said. "I did want to. I *do* want to. But that doesn't mean we should do it."

I nodded. But her words kept going around and around in my head. She did want to.

And a part of me wanted her to. That image of her pale thighs spread wide, a black lover between them. A black cock pushing its way between slippery, pink pussy lips. I could carry that image around in my head for the rest of my life. Or I could actually do something about it.

Kim was watching me, her eyes growing wider and wider as I sat there in silence. "Lewis?" she asked tentatively. "I wasn't meaning—Honey, it's okay. I wasn't—"

"What if this is our only chance?" I blurted. "I mean...we can't do this back in LA, right? We might run into someone we know. What if Harry, or Rick and Amy, saw you in a bar with no wedding ring on? What if the guy found you, somehow, after he'd...seduced you, or even slept with you?" I looked around the beach. "We're on vacation. No one here knows us. What we do here, stays here. A one-time thing."

"You mean you want me to?" She hugged her knees and laid her head on her hands as she looked at me. "You want me to sleep with him?"

My face burned. God, when she said it like that, it sounded awful.

And hot.

"Yes," I said in a tiny voice. "I think so."

We stared into each other's eyes for a moment. It was almost as if we were strangers, we'd changed so much in the last few days. And yet, at the same time, I felt as if I was truly knowing her for the first time.

"If we did this," she said hoarsely, "we would

have to be okay afterwards. You'd have to promise that you'd be okay when it was over. That you'd never hold it against me, or judge me."

"No. Of course not!"

"Are you *sure?* It's easy to say, but are you sure?"

I thought about it. I thought about how angry I'd been, when I saw his hands on her. How much worse would it be, with him fucking her? And this was Jaric...out of all the men I'd seen look at Kim and the few I'd let get close to her, he was the one who really disturbed me. He felt...wild. Dangerous. He'd taken Kim from the bar. He'd rubbed her to orgasm in a public place. What would he be like in private? And he seemed okay with me being there— what would *that* be like, having my wife's lover aware of me, maybe even talking to me while it happened?!

But I also thought about how the sex had been afterwards. And I thought about how hard my cock had been, sitting in Jaric's bar, watching them in the booth. It all came back to those images in my head, again and again. I could make them real. I could go back to the US with memories to carry with me for the rest of my life, while the evidence of what we'd done—Jaric himself—stayed safely here in Jamaica. And, however risky it felt, the thought of Kim with Jaric turned me on way more than the thought of Kim with anyone else.

"Yes," I said slowly. "Yes. I'm sure."

CHAPTER 10

I T WASN'T A LONG WALK from the beach to Jaric's bar. We walked there hand in hand and, on the way, I took a good, long look at my wife. She'd taken a shower, still in her swimsuit, at one of the freestanding beach showers, to get the sand and sunblock off her. Her hair was still wet and lay in a heavy, golden mass down her back. Her swimsuit was drying rapidly in the hot sun, but beads of water still clung to it. She'd put on a sarong to give her some modesty on her lower half, and sandals to protect her feet, but the swimsuit still drew a lot of attention as we walked. I thought she'd never looked more beautiful.

When we walked into the bar, blinking in the gloom, Jaric was nowhere to be seen. The waiter I'd seen the night before was polishing the bar. *He's not here,* I thought, relief and disappointment competing in my chest. *It's all over. We'll just walk out—*

"Jaric?" Kim asked, her voice small and tight.

The waiter grinned and nodded to an open doorway behind the bar. Rickety wooden stairs led upward.

103

Victoria Kasari

At the top of the stairs, there was no door—we just emerged into a one-room apartment. Bare brick walls, with rafters overhead. There was an old iron double bed, with white sheets and pillows, but no covers—they weren't needed, in the heat. A fan hummed quietly as it moved the air around, streamers from a long-past party still caught in its screen. The blinds were closed, leaving just a few shafts of sunlight to slice through the room.

Jaric lay on the bed, still in shorts and t-shirt, his hands behind his head. He was grinning at us.

"I knew you'd come. Sit down. Let me get you something to drink." He got up and moved past us.

There was a wooden kitchen chair beside a desk, but only one. We both shuffled towards it nervously.

Jaric clumped down the stairs, his size making the wood creak and protest. We looked at one another, but neither of us said anything. Kim was breathing fast, her pupils huge and dilated. Fight or flight. This was really going to happen, unless I did something to stop it. And I didn't want to.

My eyes fell on the desk. There were textbooks there. Legal ones. Jaric must be studying—night school, maybe, given that he seemed only a few years younger than us.

His feet, clumping up the stairs again. When he emerged, still grinning, he was carrying three cold beers. The bottles looked tiny in his huge hands. He passed one to me and one to Kim, keeping the last one for himself. "Sit down, mon," he told me, nodding at the chair. "Kim can sit with me. Over there."

And he nodded at the bed.

Gulping, I sat down in the chair. Jaric took Kim by the hand and led her over to the bed, sitting her down on the edge. The whole bed sank as his muscled body settled next to hers. Kim sat there frozen, her eyes locked on me. She took a chug of her beer. Then another.

"Relax," Jaric drawled, making the word last a full five seconds. His huge arm slid around her back and he pulled her into him. I watched as his dark fingers appeared around the edge of her waist. God, she looked so frail, next to him. The top of her head was barely past his shoulder. I looked down at his groin, and there was a bulge already there. If he was really as big as Kim had said, would she be able to take him?

I sipped my own beer as Jaric's free hand came up and stroked my wife's cheek, brushing damp strands of hair back behind her ear. Then his lips were coming down on hers and—

They were kissing, right in front of me. And this time I didn't have to steal glances or watch on the screen of my phone. This time, I could see every detail. I saw Kim tense for a second, and her eyes went to me. They stayed open as she started to kiss him...but then, as his tongue slipped inside her mouth, she gave a kind of groan and her eyelids fluttered closed. Then she was lost in it, moving with him. At first, the kiss was slow and tender, relaxing her. But as she got into it, it grew hot and heavy. The hand around her waist started to work its way over her back, stroking every inch of her, toying with the straps at her shoulders. Then he backed off a little way, making her follow him with her mouth, so that *she* was the one doing most of the work.

When Jaric finally broke the kiss, Kim was heavy-lidded and panting. Under his spell again. He motioned her to stand up.

"Now you take it off, you sweet thing. Show me what you got." He grinned at me. "And show your husband, too."

I saw Kim's legs tremble as she stood up. The sarong was first. She untied it and drew the thin fabric from her, then tossed it over the end of the bed. Her legs were smoothly pale in the dim room.

"She's got good legs—eh, Lewis? Long and sexy." Jaric reached out and grabbed her hand, pulling her towards him so that she stood just in front of him. He ran his palm up the outside of one leg, then down. Then both hands, and she trembled again. Then up the inside of her thighs, pushing her legs apart. His hand cupped her groin through her swimsuit, his thumb right over her pussy. He started to rub her there, slow and steady, and she gasped.

"I knew this one was hot for it," he told me, without taking his eyes from her body. "Soon as I saw her in that summer dress."

The blood was thundering in my ears as I watched his thick, black thumb rub at her. It was really happening. I could barely breathe.

Kim's breathing had quickened. She put her hands on his massive shoulders to steady herself as his thumb stroked up and down. I watched as she started to grind her hips in the air. Then, with his other hand, Jaric got hold of the back of her swimsuit and pulled it up, hard, between her legs. Kim caught her breath.

Jaric turned her, so that her ass was towards him, almost in his face as he sat, and her front was towards me. And now, between her thighs, I could see what he'd done to her. He'd pulled the thin, shiny fabric tight enough that it was shaped around her folds, around the narrow slit of her pussy. I could actually see the outline of her lips.

His hands wound around her body. One returned to her groin, stroking her there, and now that the fabric was so tight against her it was almost as if she was naked under his fingers. The other hand slid up to her breast, massaging it firmly. His huge hand squeezed and circled, and I could see the soft globe being squashed and lifted through the shining material. Between his fingers, her nipple slowly hardened, poking through the fabric.

I looked up at her face. She was gasping, her face red, her whole body moving sinuously in response to his fondling, a slow, hypnotic rhythm. As if he was making her dance for me. I'd never seen anything so sexy. My wife, writhing and twisting in pleasure under the hands of another man.

This is wrong! She's my wife! I knew that I should run over there and break the beer bottle over Jaric's head. Grab my wife and flee, and fuck her to make her mine again. But even as the anger built and built, my cock grew harder and harder.

"Look at her, mon. She wants to fuck. Don't you?" And he gave her a tap on the ass. Not a full-on slap, just a playful tap. But it was so unexpected that she jerked and yelped. "Y—Yes," she said.

"But it isn't your husband you want on top of you. Is it?" Jaric asked.

Kim's eyes grew wide. She looked horrified. But I stared back at her, showing her that I could take it. A part of me actually wanted to hear it.

"N—No," she managed.

Jaric grinned at both of us, victory in his eyes. "Get the damn thing off, then." He released her and she took a stumbling step away from him. Her eyes were on the floor as she unfastened her sandals and kicked them off. Then she hooked the spaghetti straps off her shoulders and started to peel the swimsuit off her body. Her breasts emerged, full and ripe and swollen with her arousal, her nipples hard as pebbles. Then the smooth flatness of her stomach. She pushed the gathered fabric further, just a rubbery tube now, rolling down her hips. The little strip of hair above her pussy came into view, gleaming in the shafts of sunlight that were coming through the window. As the swimsuit peeled lower, I saw her soft, pink lips, already gleaming with moisture. Then the thing was falling down her legs, a tangled figure-eight of red fabric, and she was pushing it away with her foot.

It hit me that this was the first time Jaric had seen her naked.

"You got a beautiful wife, Lewis," he told me. He pulled her close, again with her back to him, and slid his hands over her body once more. This time, he was touching bare skin. "She's all cold, from the sea. I'll soon warm her up." His big palms moved in circles, lazily lifting and lowering her breasts. I imagined how she must feel, her flesh cool and damp from wearing the swimsuit. I imagined how her hard nipples must feel as they grazed his palms.

I had to imagine, because it wasn't me touching her. My guts twisted.

"She's got a sweet body," Jaric told me. "Good tits." One hand slid over her tummy. "Has she given you a kid, yet? She doesn't feel like it."

"N—No," I said thickly. My voice didn't sound like my own.

He spoke to Kim. "He hasn't knocked you up yet?"

He ran his hand over her stomach again, feeling her flatness, and she gasped. "N—No," she croaked.

"What does she do for you, mon?" Jaric asked me. "She's got a body built for love." He ran one hand down her naked back and over her ass, then squeezed one cheek firmly. Then both cheeks. "She let you fuck her here?"

We'd never tried anal sex. "N—No."

"How about her mouth? She take you between those sweet lips?"

I swallowed. I'd been sipping my beer to wet my dry mouth. Only half of it was gone, yet I felt drunk. Drunk on arousal, I guess. I couldn't believe what was happening. "Yes. Sometimes."

Jaric grinned. He finally stood up and, for a second, he loomed over her. He put his mouth close to her ear. "You want to suck me, Kim?"

Kim looked me in the eye, biting her lip. Then she slowly nodded.

Jaric put his hands on her shoulders and turned her, so that they were facing each other, side-on to me. He casually lifted his t-shirt and stripped it off. Kim and I both drew in our breath as we saw him topless for the first time. His skin was a rich cocoa brown, falling off to black in the shadows. Broad, chiseled pecs stood above a tightly-defined stomach, his dark abs like a washboard. I'd been right about the tattoos. A flaming skull, with devil horns, and something that might have been the devil himself. God, his biceps were huge, even bigger than they'd looked under his t-shirt.

Kim sank to her knees. I'm not sure if she willed it, or if her legs just gave way. Maybe a little of both. She stared up at him, open-mouthed, her eyes taking in his face, his chest, his arms.

Jaric unfastened his shorts. Shoved them down along with his underwear and kicked them aside. His cock jumped out, stiffly erect, and Kim actually jerked back as if in fear...or maybe awe.

I'd never seen a black cock before. The shaft was darker than the rest of him, a deep brown-black that was a stark contrast to my wife's lightly-tanned skin. The head was gray-pink, throbbing and smooth. He was cut, I saw. And huge. The head seemed as big as a plum. That alone would fill Kim's mouth, I was sure. The shaft was at least twice as thick as mine—it seemed almost as thick as my wrist. And he was long—maybe eight or nine inches. At the base swung two heavy, dark balls that were definitely bigger than mine.

She couldn't take him. She couldn't possibly take him. We'd have to back out of the actual sex. How was she even going to take him in her mouth?!

Jaric beckoned her and she shuffled forward on her knees, her eyes locked on that huge, throbbing cock. She nervously lifted one slender hand, glancing at me as if for approval, and wrapped it around the shaft. Then she did the same with the other hand, and even then she wasn't holding all of his length.

She opened her mouth as wide as it would go and engulfed the head, managing to take all of it between her lips. She sealed them around it, just at the start of the shaft, and then I saw her cheeks hollow as she began to suck.

My wife. My wife had another man's cock in her mouth.

She's cheating on me. The thought hit me like a sledgehammer. This was different to when he'd rubbed her to orgasm. This was penetration, of a sort. It was called oral *sex* for a reason. She was cheating on me.

She's not cheating on you.

She's cheating on me!

I went back and forth, agonized. I wanted to run over there and drag her off him. And yet it was the hottest sight I'd ever seen. The image of her soft, pink lips stretched around that black shaft was burning itself into the deepest depths of my brain, never to be forgotten.

Jaric looked across at me and grinned, his teeth very white. He reached down and brushed Kim's damp hair back from her face and it was a practiced move. And that's when I knew.

He'd done this before.

"A little more, now," he told Kim. "Move your hands."

Kim started to stroke along his shaft with both hands at once. God, her fingers barely met around it! I watched as she opened her mouth wider still and tried to take more of him. She pushed forward with her head and the dark shaft sank between her lips. Her eyes were turned upward, locked on his. An inch slid into her mouth and she dropped one of her hands from his cock to give herself room. Another inch. *God!*

She started to move her head back and forth on the shaft, her breasts bouncing and swaying like ripe fruit with the movement. I could see the darker line where his cock glistened wetly from her mouth and, as he pulled back slightly, the head cleared her mouth, its bulging pinkness shining too. Her tongue chased it, licking. I glanced up at Jaric to see him looking right at me. That's why he'd pulled out. He'd wanted me to see how much she'd taken.

He pushed forward again. This time, Kim took a little more—the head and about three inches of the shaft. That filled her mouth to capacity, but still she tried to go deeper. On the next bob of her head, she gagged.

He was right at the back of her throat.

My beer was forgotten in my hand. My other hand was clutching at the edge of my chair. I could see the movements of her cheeks as her tongue worked frantically, slathering over him, swirling around him. Meanwhile, her hand stroked up and down his shaft, bringing him closer to the edge. They stayed there for long minutes, my wife naked and on her knees, her black lover standing proudly before her.

Then Jaric pushed her gently back.

"Time you got on the bed," he told her. "Let's give you what you want."

Kim turned to me, her eyes wide. This was it. Decision time.

Jaric saw our hesitation. "You want this?" he asked Kim, nodding down at his erect, shining cock.

She nodded dumbly.

Jaric turned to me. "And you—you want to see this in her?"

I caught my breath. *In her.* God, it was so crude, so base...and yet, that's exactly what I did want. I did want to see him in her. I wanted to see that black cock spread her lips and plunge inside her right up to the balls.

I nodded.

Jaric grinned and motioned her onto the bed. She sat down on the edge, then swung her legs up. Then she lay down on her back. Her lightly-tan skin looked dark at first, against the white sheets, but as soon as Jaric started to climb on, he was midnight-dark against her paleness. It was just like all the images that had flashed through my head, the contrast of their two bodies electrifying.

"Come sit closer," Jaric told me. "You want to see." It was a statement, not a question. I pulled my chair across the room, still not quite believing what I was doing. When I sat down again, I was only a foot or so from the edge of the bed. Close enough to touch my wife.

Only I wouldn't be the one touching her.

Jaric was kneeling at the end of the bed. Now he took my wife's slender ankles in his hands and lifted them, stepping them wide apart and pushing her knees up. I watched as her pussy opened to him. Inside, I could see her wetness glistening. She lay there staring up at him as he approached, her breathing quick.

He lowered himself between her spread legs, his cock bobbing stiffly. It brushed her thigh, huge and heavy, and she gasped. As he moved fully into position, he supported himself on one arm and reached down with the other to guide himself into her.

I watched the head of his cock approach her lips. *God, this is really going to happen!* Two inches away. One inch. He was about to—

"Wait!" I said in a strangled moan. "You're not wearing a condom!"

Jaric look surprised, then shrugged. "I want to feel her. And I don't have any."

And he turned back to her. I waited for Kim to join my protest, but she was just staring up at him, almost panting. *This is a bad idea,* I thought. *What if he....*

But I wanted it so badly. We both did. And we'd done the pulling out trick with me, and it had been fine. *But what if—*

Too late. With a grunt of approval, he pushed his hips forward. I watched, as if in slow motion, as the tip of his head parted her lips. As he started to slide inside, he was so wide that the lips bowed inward, and she gasped. Then, as he pushed with his hips, they gave way and he slid easily on her moisture. The head slid in, right up to its widest point.

Kim's eyes went wide. "God!" she said with a gasp. "So big!" She made little scuttling motions with her hips and ass, as if trying to move away from him. I could see her lips shining, lubricating around his girth as she moved against him. He let her move, staying exactly where he was. And, after a moment, her movements died away and she was still again. I saw her grip her sheets in both hands...and then nod.

He pushed. The head stretched her wider and wider and her mouth opened in a silent cry of disbelief—

And then the head plunged into her, her body closing after it, drum-tight around his shaft. "*God!*" Kim whispered.

"How does it feel?" I asked desperately.

Her mouth moved for a few seconds before any words came out. "Stretching—It's stretching me. God, it's so thick...."

I looked at Jaric, who was grinning, and then back at her. "Do you want to stop?"

"....nooo."

Jaric planted his other hand on the bed, so that he was braced above her. And then he started to slowly ease his length into her. I was hypnotized by the sight of his black shaft pushing slowly between those stretched pink lips. His hairless, mahogany ass cheeks moved gradually up the bed between her thighs.

My wife. My wife has another man inside her. Ever since we'd first met, I'd been her only lover. Now, a man she'd known less than a day was thrusting up into her. I didn't even know his last name. Jesus, did she?!

Kim let out a groan. I looked up at her face, flushed and gasping, and then down to the point where they joined. Jaric's cock was halfway inside her and, as I watched, he slowed to a stop. "Tight girl," he said approvingly. "You never took a big man before. Did you?"

I flushed, because *big man* implied that I

wasn't. But I'd seen his cock and I'd seen mine and I knew it was true.

Kim shook her head.

Jaric lowered himself onto his forearms and began to thrust. Each slow stroke of his cock drew a groan from my wife—not a groan of pain, but of disbelief and pleasure. Each time he thrust, her breasts bounced and rolled on her chest. And with each thrust, he moved a little deeper in her. No more than a half inch each time, but deeper. God, was he intending to go all the way in? Surely he couldn't! He wouldn't fit!

But I watched as, thrust by thrust, my wife was inexorably filled. His balls were bouncing and jiggling down at his root, and it was no more than three inches from her lips, now. I watched them come closer and closer.

"I—God, I—" Kim was panting. "I don't know if I—"

"Too much?" I asked quickly. "Is he too big?"

"You'll handle it just fine," Jaric told her. "You'll squeeze out a baby one day soon. You can take me."

Kim twisted her head on the pillow to look at me. On instinct, I reached out and brushed the hair from her forehead. She was damp with sweat.

"Do you want to stop?" I asked.

She hesitated for a split second, then shook her head. "No. It feels...God, he's stretching me...but it feels...Ah! It feels really really good."

Something cold clutched around my heart...but at the same time, a throb of heat went straight down to my groin. "Okay," I whispered.

Jaric moved his hands again, putting them on her shoulders, now. That made her look even more fragile, with his strong fingers curled around them. He thrust harder, driving more and more of him into her, her breasts bouncing between them. "God!" said Kim. "God! I—"

And then, with a groan, Jaric pushed hard against her and I saw that he'd hilted himself. His balls were resting against her ass.

"Ah!" It was almost a little scream. Kim's hands were frantic at the sheets, grabbing and twisting them into sweaty hillocks. "God! That's—"

"What? Does it hurt?"

"N—No! It's—God...It's wonderful. I can feel him...God, right up inside me. *Right* up. I think—I think he's touching me places I've never been touched before."

Places she'd never been touched before. Places *I'd* never touched her.

Places I never would.

Would it ever be the same between us, after this? Would *she* even be the same? *God, he must be stretching her, with that huge cock....*

He bent down and kissed her neck, nibbling her there, and she tossed her head on the pillow. He ground his pelvis against hers and she let out a growl as his cock moved inside her.

And then he drew back a little and looked at her, waiting.

At first, she just lay there, getting used to his size inside her. Then there was a tiny movement of her hips. A humping towards him. Then, as he still refused to move, she started to gasp and plead. "Please," she begged. "Please."

Jaric glanced across at me. He didn't have to say anything. My face was already red, my cock already hard. That was my wife, begging him to fuck her.

And he was only too happy to oblige.

He moved his hands to her breasts, using his knees to take some of his weight so that he didn't crush her, and began to squeeze them as he fucked her. He was a little rougher with her than I would have been, and I was shocked to see Kim hiss with pleasure in response.

His thrusts were only a few inches long at first, but they quickly got longer. I watched, transfixed, as that slippery, dark length moved out of her and then slammed back in. Four inches, five. Seven, eight. Soon he was fucking her with the whole length, only the head remaining inside her.

"Yes!" said Kim, a sharp little cry. "God, yes!"

Her head started to roll back against the pillow, her chin going to the ceiling. Her eyes screwed tight, the pleasure overwhelming her. His cock was slamming into her, now, thrust after thrust, his heavy balls slapping against her ass with each stroke. His fingers were digging deep into the soft flesh of her breasts, his thumbs rubbing her nipples. I sat forward in my chair. She was going to—God, she was going to—

"*Yes!*" shrieked Kim. "*Yes! Faster! More!*"

Jaric sped up, the whole bed shaking with the force of his strokes. The head of it was banging against the wall. Kim's feet lifted off the bed and her legs wrapped around him. I held my breath. It was an even more powerful image than the one I'd had in my head. My white wife, not only fucked by her black lover but pulling him to her, her pale ankles tight under his ass cheeks.

Jaric's mouth was drawn into a savage snarl. His hands squeezed her breasts, his mouth moved back to her throat—

"*YES!*" screamed Kim. And she went stiff under him, her legs gripping him tight. I imagined her pussy, squeezing rhythmically around him. Her fingers clutched at the sheets, white-knuckled, and she sucked in air through a narrow gap between her clenched teeth.

I saw a spasm pass down her body, her spine arching as it passed. She trembled for a second, and then she was slumping on the bed, spent.

Jaric smiled down at her.

And then he withdrew from her, and patted her on the rump, indicating that she should turn over. It wasn't over.

Kim climbed shakily to her hands and knees. Jaric moved her so that she was facing me, with her knees on the edge of the bed. He stood and moved behind her, spreading her thighs apart. I glimpsed his cock, iron-hard and shining with her wetness. Then he buried himself in her from behind.

"Ah!" Kim gasped as he went balls-deep on his first thrust. "God!"

I caught my breath. *God, this is amazing! But I shouldn't be—Why am I turned on by—*

Jaric drew slowly out and then slid back in. In this position, he could go deeper into her. Perhaps only a half inch, but it was enough to make a difference. Kim was looking right at me when he went all the way in for the first time, and her eyes snapped wide.

He started to thrust and, at the end of each stroke, she gave a high little cry as he pressed up against the very limits of her. "God! He's—Lewis, he's so...*big!* He's filling me! He's filling me and filling me!"

Jaric had hold of her hips now, his fingers starkly black against her skin. He started to hammer into her in a steady rhythm. I leaned forward in my chair, my wife's face only inches from my own.

"Ah! Ah! Oh God, it's—It's so good! He's so deep and it's—Ah!—It's so good!" Her mouth was wide, her eyes wild. "*God!*"

My cock had been painfully hard in my shorts this entire time. It was too much. I finally took it out and started to stroke it. I was already close.

Jaric's rhythm sped up. Kim cried out again, then again as Jaric reached down with one hand and started to play with her hanging breasts. "God! I'm going to—I'm coming again!"

I was frantically stroking myself now. She was going to come, right in front of me! I heard Jaric, behind her, give a grunt. He was going to come, too.

God! *He was going to come!*

You now have a choice of endings.

If you want Jaric to pull out in time, keep reading.

If you want Jaric to stay exactly where he is, turn to page 131.

Victoria Kasari

ENDING A

KIM BEGAN TO SHUDDER, her eyes rolling back, her back arching. She pushed her hips back towards her lover and *shook,* and I knew that inside her, her walls would be clutching and spasming around his cock, almost milking him—

At that second, Jaric withdrew and, to my immense relief, his cock was shining with her juices but showed no signs of his own seed. He stroked his massive shaft once, twice—

And then he was shooting, long hot ropes of cum flying through the air to land on Kim's upraised rump and the small of her back. She let out a cry as she felt it land, still shuddering and writhing through her own release. Her breasts tossed and swayed. Her mouth hung open as she gasped.

My wife. Trembling in orgasm as she was bathed in the cum of another man. On all fours on a stranger's bed, her body still aching from taking his huge length—

The heat was raging through me. Anger and

lust twisted into one. My hand was still on my cock and it took only a few strokes before I, too, was shooting, my seed coating her shoulders and upper back.

And then all of us were standing there, panting.

Kim slowly slumped to the bed and lay on her side, her body sticky and glistening with our combined load. She closed her eyes and just stayed there for a while, returning from her high.

I hauled up my pants and turned to Jaric. *Another few seconds....* "You—You nearly—God, you nearly—"

Jaric picked up his beer, not bothering to put his clothes back on. "Relax, mon. I pulled it out in time. Kim ain't gonna be swelling up—not with my baby, at least." He looked me dead in the eye as he said it, grinning. What the hell did he mean by that?

I looked down at Kim. "Are you...okay?"

She groggily opened her eyes...then smiled. "Okay? I'm better than okay. That was...wow."

I knew I was being paranoid, but—"And he definitely pulled out in time? None of it—"

She shook her head and gave me a condescending look. "No," she said, as if humoring me. "None of it's inside me." I detected just a hint of disappointment in her voice and, at the end of the sentence, she glanced across at Jaric, almost unconsciously.

She'd wanted him to come inside her. The realization slammed into me. Both of them had wanted it.

"We should go," I said thickly. It terrified me how close we'd come.

Jaric, being Jaric, didn't get dressed. He sprawled on the bed, his cock huge even as it softened, while Kim cleaned herself in his bathroom and then pulled her clothes on. Her swimsuit was still damp and she shuddered as the cool fabric touched her body.

When she was ready, Jaric finally stood up and she gave him a hug. Then a peck on the cheek.

He raised an eyebrow in a *that-won't-do* way.

I tensed as he pulled her into a deep kiss, his naked body against her clothed one. Her breasts squashed against him through the swimsuit. Her mouth opened wide, his tongue deep inside her. What started out as a goodbye had quickly turned into something else.

I saw her nipples begin to harden through the fabric of her swimsuit. I saw Jaric's cock twitch and begin to rise.

Kim pulled herself from him, panting and red-faced. She glanced at me, then looked away, shame-faced.

Jaric was grinning as I shook his hand. "You come back anytime, mon," he told us.

We walked down the stairs slowly, neither of us saying anything. When we reached the bar, the place had filled up a little. And everyone there was grinning at us.

There was no door on Jaric's one-room apartment. They'd all heard Kim having sex. Most of the regulars probably knew Jaric. They knew exactly what had just happened, and that I must be the husband. They knew that I'd just sat there and watched my wife be—

I marched through the bar, looking straight ahead, towing Kim by one hand. I can barely put into words what I was feeling. It felt so utterly wrong—I'd just allowed another man to seduce, fuck...almost *impregnate* my wife. And yet....

And yet in some weird way, it felt *right*. It had been the most erotic experience of my life. I only had to close my eyes and it was happening right there in front of me. Every glimpse of black skin on white, every noise she'd made. The memories would be there for life.

I looked at my gorgeous wife and realized that in some way, on some level...*this is where I'm supposed to be*. This was my proper role. My stomach lurched. What did that make me? Some sort of cuckold? Was this going to be our sex lives, now—me watching her with other men? Terrifyingly, that didn't seem all that bad, to one part of me. But the rest of me was rebelling, wanting this to be a one-time thing, wanting to go back to normal.

What if there was no "normal," anymore. Kim had had Jaric, now. What if she didn't want me?

I blundered out of the bar and down the street, barely looking where I was going. Kim squeezed my hand a few times, and when I glanced at her she was looking at me nervously, wondering if I was going to go ape again as I had before. But it wasn't anger I was feeling. Now I felt...hollow. As if there wasn't any of *me* left. If another man fucked my wife instead of me, was I good for anything?

We walked and walked, still in silence, until we came to a small harbor filled with fishing boats. The place was mostly deserted. I started to wander along the dock, still lost in thought.

"Lewis?" Kim asked. "Talk to me."

I stopped and turned back to look at her. We were standing next to an eggshell-blue fishing boat, its name so faded I could barely make it out. Old ropes and nets littered the deck.

"What happens now?" I asked.

Her voice was strained. "What do you want to happen now?"

My heart ached. So things *were* different. We'd changed them. I stared at her. "Do you still want me?"

She blinked. "Do I still—Of course I still want you! Do you still want me?"

I stared at her. "Why would I not want you?"

She looked at her feet. "Because you saw me...behaving like that. Wanting Jaric so much. Coming my brains out. Do you think I'm a slut?"

I grabbed her arms. "God, *no!* That was the sexiest thing I've ever seen!"

She looked up at me. "Really?"

"Really. Why would you think—"

"You've been so quiet," she said. "We've been walking for hours—I thought I'd ruined everything by fucking him."

"I thought *I'd* ruined everything—" I took a deep breath. "Do you want to do this again?"

Her mouth moved a few times but no words came out. "Yes," she said at last. "But only if you do, too."

"I think I do. Not immediately, but soon. But"—here was the big question—"do you still want me as well?"

She pulled me close. "Yes!"

We clutched each other for a moment. Then I asked, "At the end, when he was about to come...you sort of wanted him to come inside you. Didn't you?"

She shook her head. Then nodded. "Sort of," she said, her eyes going to the floor again. "I don't know why. I think nature took over. I *did* want to feel it inside me." She pressed her lips together into a tight line and then nodded. "I wanted to get pregnant by him. I mean, just as a crazy, fleeting thought. But I did."

I stared at her, feeling the anger rise. But it was a very specific sort of anger, a sort I could control.

And something else was rising, too.

"You wanted his baby?" I asked, my voice tight.

She grabbed my upper arms. "Only for a moment," she said quickly. "Just for a second. I don't want his. I want yours."

I put an arm around her waist and picked her up. "You're going to get it," I told her. And carried her onto the fishing boat.

"W—What are you—" But she didn't try to stop me as I carried her aboard. And she didn't protest as I laid her down on the coils of rope, the pile making her arch her back slightly, her hips raised.

I could hear the blood rushing in my ears. Nature had taken over, she'd said, while he was inside her. Well, now nature was taking over again. I was going to reclaim her. In the most basic way possible.

I started undoing my belt.

"H—Honey?" she asked. "What are you—"

"I'm going to fuck you," I said, freeing my stiff cock. "And you're going to have my child."

Her eyes went wide. "Your—" She stared at my erect cock. "But—We were going to wait until we were—"

"No more waiting." I grabbed the crotch of her swimsuit and pulled it to the side. We were completely exposed to anyone looking down into the harbor, the side of the boat providing almost no privacy at all. Her naked pussy gleamed in the daylight, her folds still wet. I knelt between her legs, holding the fabric away from her. But I paused at the last second and locked eyes with her. Giving her the choice.

She was as turned on as I was, almost panting at the idea. Her eyes were gleaming.

She nodded.

I thrust into her in one long push, the heat of her taking me by surprise. Her position on the ropes presented her perfectly to me—hips lifted, her upper body tilted slightly away. I went deep on my first thrust, then started to pound at her. Her walls were silky smooth and tight around me.

She looked up at me, amazed. And I knew why she wore that expression—I felt harder and, crazily, *bigger* than I ever had. It made no sense. I should have felt small, after Jaric's huge size. I should have felt inferior. I should have been worried about whether she was stretched, whether she could even feel me. But it wasn't like that at all. It felt *great,* and I felt like a returning king. Claiming my woman.

Breeding my woman.

I put my hands on her shoulders, pinning her in place as I rammed into her. "Is this what you want?" I gasped. *"Is this what you want?!"*

She was panting, looking up at me in astonishment. I could feel her getting even wetter around me. "God, yes!" she croaked. "Like that. Fuck me!"

My hands went to her breasts, squeezing hard, my fingers digging into the soft flesh. She bucked and moaned under me, grinding up against me. I'd never been rough with her before. I'd had no idea that she liked it, until I'd seen her with Jaric.

"You're mine!" I told her, almost yelling it. The red mist had come down. All I could see was her face in front of me, her wide eyes looking up at me. I hammered into her even harder, my cock filling her again and again. I could feel the climax rushing up inside me and, incredibly, I could feel her start to writhe and twist under me, too. I'd never known Kim to come so fast.

My balls started to tighten. "I'm going to fill you up," I told her. "I don't care if we're not ready. I'm going to shoot inside you and knock you up, right now!"

"Yes!" she said in a strangled moan. "Yes!"

And then her heat was squeezing and spasming around me, her fingers digging into my back, and I drove all the way inside her and my cock was leaping and spurting in her depths. Jet after jet of hot cum shot from me and, as she shuddered in orgasm, she went tense in response to each squirt. It felt like nothing I'd ever experienced...even better than watching her and Jaric. She was my princess, carried off by the rival king, and now I'd brought her home and made her mine again. I didn't feel jealous anymore. I felt victorious.

And I suddenly understood Jaric's comment, when he said she would swell up with *his* baby. He'd known this would happen.

Kim clutched me tight as my spurts came to an end, and then we lay there, locked so tightly together we were almost one body. I gazed down at her, panting, and I realized that this is how I wanted it to be. Showing her off. Sharing her. And then making her mine again.

That was the best feeling in the world.

"I didn't want to interrupt," said a deep, Jamaican voice from behind us. "But if you're finished, I have to get the boat out."

My head craned round. A Jamaican fisherman in his sixties was grinning down at us from the gangplank.

I hugged Kim tight and, together, we laughed.

***

I was worried, of course. It's in my nature. When we discovered that Kim was pregnant, we knew that it must have happened in Jamaica. And while Jaric had pulled out, many a teenage mother will confirm to you that the withdrawal method isn't 100%.

We talked options but there was only really one. We knew in our hearts that everything would be okay. So I watched as my beautiful wife blossomed into pregnancy, her breasts becoming larger and heavier. That trim, toned stomach swelled into a ball and then into a full, swollen belly, and I never grew tired of running my hand over it, just as Jaric had done.

In the early months, there was plenty of time for sex. We didn't have sex with anyone else, but we talked about it a lot, getting off on memories of what we'd done and making plans of what we might do next time. We started to investigate adult dating sites and talked about creating a profile. We both agreed we wanted to do it again. Carefully and discreetly, but we wanted to do it, once Kim had had the baby and was ready. In the meantime, we enjoyed each other's bodies again and again.

We'd both learned a lot about ourselves—what makes us tick, what we enjoy in bed. We were both better lovers thanks to Jamaica. Kim didn't feel shy about asking for what she wanted and I knew better how to please her. Weirdly, her being pregnant was a huge sexual kick for both of us. If we'd stuck to our original plans, I knew that getting her pregnant would have been an efficient, but ultimately sterile experience, all calendars and plotting temperatures on graphs. But the way we'd done it, every time I looked at her bump, I felt like a million bucks. I'd gotten her pregnant. I'd succeeded where another man had failed. There was no feeling like it in the world.

***

If I told you there wasn't a moment of concern in the delivery room, I'd be lying. We could have done a paternity test, of course, but we agreed not to—because if it was Jaric's baby, what then? So although I knew in theory that it was going to be mine, Kim and I still gripped each other's hands extra tight as the baby emerged.

It was a boy. He was white, and he had my eyes and Kim's smile.

I'd thought that Jamaica was going to be a one-off adventure—something that we left behind when we flew home. Yet it gave us the greatest gift we could receive, and changed our lives forever. Once the baby was a little older, once Kim felt ready...

Well, who knows what adventures we'd have?

ENDING B

"Pull out!" I yelled. "She isn't on the pill!"

Jaric ignored me, either not registering it or not caring.

"Tell him!" I said, right in Kim's ear. "Tell him he has to pull out!"

But Kim had her eyes shut, now, her body already starting to spasm and buck.

My hard cock slipped from my hand. I ran at Jaric, trying to push him from her, but it was like pushing at a stone statue. "Stop!" I begged. "You'll get her pregnant!"

Jaric took the hand that was on Kim's breasts, slid it down to her stomach and rubbed her there. As I remembered he'd done before.

"No!" I shouted.

"Ah!" Kim threw her head back as she came, tensing and shaking. I imagined her pussy, spasming and clutching around his shaft. Irresistible.

Jaric gave a groan, slapped both hands onto Kim's hips and buried himself deep inside her. I imagined that thick head sliding right the way up against her cervix—

"No!" I whispered. And suddenly, my hand was back on my cock, stroking.

I watched in horror as Jaric's hips began to jerk, and suddenly Kim's eyes snapped open. She was twisting and shuddering, her orgasm stretching out and out, extended by what was happening inside her. "He's coming!" she shouted. "God, he's coming, right inside me! Lewis! I can feel him, he's—he's filling me up!"

And my cock was jumping and spurting in my hand, sending long ropes of cum across her back. Behind her, Jaric's balls were tight up against the base of his cock, firing spurt after spurt of thick cum right up into her fertile cavern.

There was silence as the three of us all crested our peak...and then slowly descended.

At last, Jaric stepped back. I pushed past him, and there in front of me was the evidence of what he'd done. Kim's pussy was gaping wide, and I could see right up into her depths. The wet pinkness was filled with creamy white, and only a small dribble of it was oozing back out. The rest was doing its work inside her.

Kim closed her thighs and rolled onto her back, flopping on the bed. Jaric picked up his shorts and started to pull them on.

I stumbled away from them, aghast. My shorts were still tangled around one leg. I pulled them up over my softening cock. *What had we done?!*

My wife lay naked on Jaric's bed, breathing hard. Her entire body was coated in a thin layer of sweat and, between her legs, she was sticky with his seed. I put my hands to my head. As before, now that the heat was gone, reality was setting in. I'd let another man fuck my wife! Right in front of me! And there was a very good chance that she might now be pregnant.

"Calm down, mon," Jaric told me. "You got to relax. Have a beer."

He passed me the bottle, but I slapped it out of his hand. It didn't break, but it hit the floor and rolled, glugging its contents across the floor. "We're leaving," I croaked, and grabbed Kim's hand. Something was wrong. She was heavy-lidded, almost semi-conscious. Jesus, had he drugged her, somehow?! "What's wrong with her?"

"Nothing, mon. She just never came like that before. Married women never have."

I stared at him. And finally worked it out. "You knew she was married, didn't you? You saw the ring, that first time, when she was sitting alone and I was up on the balcony. All that time in the bar...in the booth...you knew she was married. You knew I was her husband."

Jaric smiled and nodded. "You think you two are the first to play this game?"

Kim opened her eyes and let me help her to her feet, still groggy.

"There's no rush. Take it easy," Jaric told us.

But something else was bothering me. All those times he'd rubbed her stomach. He'd known she was married. He must have suspected she wasn't on birth control. "You *wanted* to get her pregnant?!" I asked in horror.

Jaric shrugged. "It's Jah will, mon. It happens or doesn't happen. It's nature." But there was a glint in his eye.

When this started, I'd thought we were playing a game. Duping local men into thinking Kim was single, then snatching her away at the last moment. But all the time, he'd been playing me. He'd spotted Kim on her own at the table, seen her ring, probably seen me when I raced downstairs to rejoin her. He'd approached her at the bar, taken her to his place next door, probably laughed to himself at my inept attempts to follow covertly. All along, he'd known it would come to this. He'd been able to play the waiting game, because he'd known what Kim wanted. What *I* had wanted. And he'd used all that to get what *he* wanted.

To get the beautiful, blonde, married American knocked up.

"Come on," I told Kim hoarsely. "We're getting out of here."

I helped her into her swimsuit. Almost immediately that she pulled it on, the crotch darkened as the cum started to trickle from her. I groaned in dismay and wrapped the sarong around her, then found her shoes.

"You come back," Jaric told Kim. "With or without him. I don't mind. Come back when you need more."

I glared at him, but Kim just looked stupefied. I led her down the stairs to the bar.

As we reached the bottom, there was laughter and cheers. Everyone was staring at us, some of them applauding. It hit me that there was no door on Jaric's tiny apartment. They'd all have heard the rhythmic thump of the bed head hitting the wall. Kim's screams of orgasm. My pleas that she might get pregnant.

We walked through the crowd, faces red. I wondered how many other couples had been in this same bar, had done this same walk of shame. I caught the eye of the waiter and he, too, was grinning. I remembered what he'd said the night before, looking at my wife. *He's a lucky guy.* Had he, too, known I was her husband? Had he known what was going to happen?

I pulled Kim outside and, in the fresh air, tried

to breathe.

Kim was staring at me, worried. There were tears in her eyes. "You promised you'd be okay afterwards," she said. "You promised."

What had we done?!

***

I walked Kim back to the hotel, trying to convince her I wasn't angry while trying to contain my rage.

I wasn't even sure who I was mad at.

Jaric? He'd done exactly what he'd said he'd do, at every stage. He hadn't hurt us or done anything against our will. Hell, we'd asked him to do it.

No. It was me I was angry at.

I was married to a wonderful woman who I loved and, just because of some stupid fantasy, I'd thrown us into a game that had now gone dangerously wrong. Why hadn't I just been satisfied with what I'd had?

But then I looked across at Kim as we walked and some of the anger drained from me. It wasn't just me. She'd had secret desires, too. Maybe, if I'd never started this, they'd never have come to the surface...but would that be good, or bad? We both were what we were, for better or worse. We had this stuff inside us. If we'd kept hiding it our entire lives...was *that* right?

Just outside our hotel, next to the fountain, I stopped and turned Kim to me. "Stop," I said. "I can't even wait until we get up to the room. I need to say this now. I'm sorry."

She'd started crying. I reached up and wiped the tears from her cheek. "I'm an idiot," I told her. "I just felt so...guilty."

"You don't need to," she told me. "You didn't make me do anything. I wanted to do it."

I shook my head. My deepest fear, the one that had been hiding under the surface the entire time, came bubbling up. "I mean, guilty that..." *That I'm not a real man,* I thought. But I couldn't say it. "That I get off on it," I said lamely.

"Who wouldn't get off on it? It was hot. God, I wish we had a movie of it. I'd love to see how he looked, fucking me." Then she caught herself and blushed.

I blinked. Even after all this, she could still surprise me. She caught my expression and giggled. I leaned forward and touched my forehead to hers. My big concern still hadn't been answered—I couldn't find a way to put it into words. But she'd reminded me of how much I loved her, and that was what was really important. We'd figure the rest out.

"Look," I said slowly, "this is going to be okay. Just...give me a while, okay? It's...I just can't believe what we did."

She nodded. "I know. But...you're not mad with me?"

"No. I'm not mad with you. We do need to do something about...you know. He came inside you."

She gave an odd little shudder at that. "I know," she said.

***

When we'd showered and put on fresh clothes, I felt a lot better. Now we just had to get her the morning-after pill. Finding it was surprisingly easy. A quick trip to a pharmacy, a couple of questions and she had the little white box in her hand. I handed her a bottle of water and watched as she put the pill in her mouth.

"I *am* going to take it, you know," she said wryly. "You don't have to stand over me."

I felt myself flush. Of course, I trusted her. But I'd be lying if I said I didn't feel better, actually seeing the pill go down. It felt like a weight had been lifted. Now the whole thing was really over, and all we had to worry about was *us*.

***

Neither of us wanted to stay cooped up in our hotel room, so we found a bar—far from Jaric's— where we could sit off in a corner, private and undisturbed. And say what we needed to say.

"You go first," she said. She'd bought a cocktail and now sat staring at it, not drinking.

I drew in a long breath. "I'm sorry," I said. "I'm sorry I freaked...*again.*" I think..." I scratched my head. "I think maybe it's built in. The caveman response. I think men just naturally freak, a bit. It's part of it." On the other hand, I noticed the anger was fading faster, this time. At least some of my rage had really been worry over the pregnancy risk and, now that was gone, I was a lot calmer.

I wasn't sure how I felt about that. Did it mean I was actually accepting things? That eventually, if we did this often enough, I wouldn't be angry at all? Would we even do this again? God, was this going to be a regular thing?!

"Did you like it?" Kim asked.

And that's what it really came down to. I drew in another long breath, considering. I already knew the answer. The question was, was I going to tell the truth?

Ever since this had started, I think I'd been worried about this moment. About what would happen if she actually fucked another man, and I had to admit that I liked it. Because I didn't know what would follow...again, I asked myself the question: what would the admission make me? And would it give her carte blanche to do it again?

I was terrified of saying it. But what else was I going to do? Lie to my wife?

I took a deep breath. "Yes," I said. "Watching you with him...was the hottest thing I've ever seen." I looked at her. "Did you?"

She hesitated, then nodded. "Yes. God, yes. It was amazing."

I couldn't help it. "Better than me?"

She sighed and started to speak.

"If you say something about Lamborghinis again—" I interrupted.

She gave me a look and I quietened down. "It *is* kind of like that, though," she said carefully. "*Different*. I wouldn't want it every day." She looked at me seriously. "I want *you* every day. But once in a while...."

We lapsed into silence.

"How did it feel?" I asked at last. I looked around us to check that no one was listening. "When he came inside you?"

She lowered her eyes.

"You liked it, didn't you?" I asked.

She flushed. "I can't explain it. It felt good. No, it felt great...the sensation of it spurting inside me. But more than that..."

I could feel the rage rising inside me again. "You wanted him to get you pregnant?"

"No! Of course not. But...I don't know. Maybe I did." She sipped her drink, thinking before she continued. "I can't explain it. Knowing I wasn't protected. Knowing it could be happening, *right then*...there was just something really primitive about it." She finally lifted her eyes to meet mine. "Maybe it's like you said. Caveman instinct. You're wired to get angry when you see someone with your woman—even if you like it. I'm wired to get extra horny when a man might be knocking me up. Especially when he's—"

She bit back her words, but I already knew what she was going to say. "An alpha male?" I asked bitterly.

She winced and looked apologetically at me, but nodded. I fumed, but I couldn't hate her for being honest. And this time, I voiced my concern out loud. "What does it make me, though?" I said. "If he's the alpha male, and I get off on seeing him with you, then what am—"

Kim put her hand on mine. "What does it matter? Why do we have to give it a name? The only thing that's important is that *I love you*. Whatever you are. I love you just the way you are."

I looked at her, stunned. And realized she was right.

"God," she said. "Can you believe we did that? I mean, *we did it?* And...I mean...we're okay...right?"

I slowly nodded. I was still all mixed up inside but, with the worry and self-hate fading, the lust was coming back. The memories of what we'd done. The sight of her, pale and writhing under her black lover. The sound she'd made when she'd come. *God.* Those memories would last a lifetime. And just as importantly, they were making me hot *now*.

"Yeah," I said. "Yeah, we're okay." I smiled and took a long look at my wife. God, she was beautiful. She'd thrown on another summer dress, a green one, this time. Her cleavage was mouth-wateringly presented by the neckline. Glancing under the table, her long, tanned legs were shapely and perfect, revealed by the knee-length skirt. Her blonde hair hung in soft waves down her back. I'd seen her take another man, seen her spread her legs and welcome him in, seen her pull him deeper into her with her ankles behind his ass. And I still loved her. If anything, I loved her more.

We'd done it. We'd lived out our fantasies and we'd gotten away with it. We still loved each other. Nothing bad had happened. The rage had dissipated, to be replaced by lust. A very specific sort of lust.

There was something I needed to do.

"Let's find the restroom," I said. And took her hand.

She frowned at me. "Together?" Then realization spread across her face. "*Oh!*"

***

Moments later, we were in the men's restroom. Kim had her back against the wall, hanging onto the sink on one side of her and the hand dryer on the other. I had her dress hiked up to her waist.

"Spread your legs," I told her in a low growl. "I'm going to fuck him out of you."

She obediently opened her thighs. Her black panties stretched tight across her mound.

I hooked my hand in them and ripped them from her. She let out a high, quick, cry.

I pushed two fingers up into her. She was as wet as I'd ever known her. I unfastened my shorts and let them fall around my thighs, not even stopping to take them off. I turned to look at the condom machine.

"You don't need one," Kim panted. "I took the pill."

My heart leapt. God, she was right. With another growl, I took my cock in my hand, positioned myself and thrust deep into her.

She let out a moan of release and clutched me to her, her head on my shoulder. Her breasts pillowed against my chest. Was she as tight as before? Had he changed her? She was so wet, it was difficult to tell. Either way, she felt amazing. Hot and slippery and writhing around me. "You're mine," I told her. "Mine. I'm going to fuck him out of you."

"Yes—"

"Fuck him right out of you," I hissed in her ear. I was thrusting hard, driving up into her hot, clinging tunnel, and I knew neither of us was going to last long. I slid my hands behind her ass, cupping her cheeks as I slammed into her, crushing her between me and the wall, and her thighs squeezed around my body as she hooked her feet behind me.

"Yes!" she said in a tight little voice. "Yes! Do it! Come inside me! Fuck him right out of me!"

I thrust even faster, even harder. The feel of her was incredible, liquid silk around my cock. "Say you're mine!" I said, half-yelling it.

"I'm yours! God, I'm yo—OOORS!"

She came, spasming and shuddering around me, and suddenly I was shooting into her depths, long hot streams of it filling her. Marking her. Reclaiming her as my own.

She slowly opened her eyes as we came down from it. Her legs slid down my body and she stepped down to the floor.

And then we were kissing, long and deep. Someone tried to open the door to come in, and I slammed it closed again with my elbow, and we both looked at each other and laughed.

***

Victoria Kasari

TWO WEEKS LATER
LOS ANGELES

"I don't understand," I said weakly. "It's not possible."

Kim showed me the pregnancy test, with its little blue line. Her face was strangely emotionless. "That's the third one. They're all the same."

I shook my head. "But you took the pill!"

"*I know I took the pill!* I don't know what happened!"

I felt as if I was going to be sick. "So it's...it's—"

"Not necessarily." She caught my eye. "Remember the restroom? It could be yours."

I took her hands. "Honey, we can't—What if it's *Jaric's?!*"

"What if it's *yours?*"

"But..."

She shook her head. "I've thought about it. I'm keeping the baby. We can make a decision after the birth."

"The *birth...!*" I looked around for the waste basket. I actually thought I was going to vomit. "You want to...we'll have to—" I stared at her tummy, still smooth and perfect. *For now.*

She looked as if she might cry. "You still— We're still—You still love me. Right?"

I threw my arms around her. "Of course! Of course I do!" I squeezed her close. And thought about the new life growing inside her, the one that could well be fathered by another man.

I'd thought we'd gotten away with it. I'd thought we'd left all evidence of our game in Jamaica. But now, maybe, our lives were irreparably changed.

Or maybe everything was fine. Maybe we'd just started our family a few months early. That was the problem: we had no way of knowing.

"We could do a test," I said, still clutching her close.

"No—"

"They can do tests! They can find out if it's mine—"

"*No!*" She pushed me back, so that she could look me in the eye. "Because what if it isn't? Then what? Then you'll...you'll want me to—Even if you didn't say anything, I'd feel like I had to—" She shook her head. "It's not the baby's fault!"

I took a deep breath, trying to stay calm. I stared at my wife. I had no idea what we were going to do, or how we were going to get through this.

All I knew was that I loved her.

I slipped my arms around her again and pulled her to me. "Okay," I said softly. "Okay."

***

I watched as Kim slowly blossomed into pregnancy. As the months passed, her breasts, already full and ripe, grew larger and heavier. Her stomach slowly swelled, first into a tight balloon, then into a big, heavy, swollen belly, the skin tight as a drum. It was going to be a big baby—that much was obvious. And I was afraid of what that meant, given my and Jaric's relative sizes.

Her skin took on a glow and her hair shone. She was more beautiful than ever. Everyone commented on how radiant she looked, and congratulated me. And I thanked them and agreed that she looked great, and knew every time that in just a few weeks I could be utterly humiliated, exposed as the man who'd let his wife sleep with another. Who'd watched a guy impregnate her, right in front of him.

We solved the mystery of the failed morning after pill, after showing the empty box to Kim's obstetrician. The pill had been a high-quality fake, manufactured in some country called San Relando and sold around the world to make a quick buck for some enterprising criminal.

I watched my wife get bigger and bigger, told her daily how beautiful she was, and hoped against hope that things would work out okay.

***

"Push, Mrs. Selman. Push!"

"*Nggghhh!*"

Kim lay on her back, one hand clenching mine painfully tight. The doctors and nurses were laughing and chatting. It had been a textbook pregnancy, and this was looking like a textbook delivery. Everyone was relaxed.

Everyone except Kim and me.

"Okay! I can see the baby's head!" called Kim's obstetrician. "Wait for the next contraction."

I looked down at my wife. Her hair was plastered to her forehead with sweat. I brushed it aside for her...and remembered the last time I'd done that, as she lay on Jaric's bed.

"Whatever happens," she breathed, "remember I love you."

I nodded, a lump in my throat. "Whatever happens," I whispered, "I love you, too."

Another contraction started. Kim gripped my hand tight. "This is it! Push, Mrs. Selman! *Push!*"

"*Nggghhh!*"

"*Push push push!*"

It all happened very fast. I leaned down to see the baby, but Kim yanked on my arm and pulled me back. Then the doctors were between me and it, wrapping it in a blanket and cutting the cord.

The obstetrician gently placed the baby at Kim's breast. "Congratulations, Mrs. Selman," she said. "You have a beautiful baby boy."

I looked down. The baby had Kim's smile.

And Jaric's black skin.

I could already see the adoration in Kim's eyes. She wasn't going to give the baby up for adoption: no way. We were going to take him home, and everyone was going to know exactly what had happened. And soon, we'd have to either invite Jaric to the US or fly out to Jamaica so that he could see his son. And when he and Kim met again, I knew our one-time adventure was going to continue right where it left off.

My life had just changed. Forever.

FROM THE AUTHOR

Thank you for reading! :) If you enjoyed this book, please consider leaving a review on Amazon. It really helps readers to find stories they'll like!

Most of my books are unfortunately only available as ebooks at the present time. However, did you know that you don't need an ereader or tablet to enjoy ebooks? Amazon's Cloud Reader lets you read them right in your web browser. They're also much cheaper than paperbacks – typically just $2.99.

But it gets better. Each time I release one, I price it at $0.99 for the first 24 hours. My mailing list subscribers get an email so they can snap it up cheap from their choice of retailer before the price goes up. To get on the list, sign up here: (you must be over 18). There's no spam, just one mail per story.

http://list.victoriakasari.com

If you liked this book, you'd probably also like my Cuckolded books. What follows is an extract from "Cuckolded – My Wife on the Oil Rig."

I love to hear from my readers!
victoriakasari@gmail.com

AN EXTRACT FROM:
CUCKOLDED
MY WIFE ON THE OIL RIG

Three weeks on an oil rig, and she'd be the only woman on board. I wasn't worried at all: my wife was completely faithful. In fact, I even encouraged her to tease the oil workers while I watched via webcam.

Then things went horribly wrong. The head of the rig hacked my laptop and, pretending to be me, encouraged my wife to go further and further with him and his buddies. Thousands of miles away, all I could do was watch in horror as they took her again and again....

In this extract, Lance—head honcho on the rig— has taken control of our hero, Glen's laptop. Glen's wife Heather believes her husband has just given her permission to sleep with Tony, one of the rig workers...she doesn't know she's actually talking to

Lance. All her husband can do is watch in horror....

Heather leaned over the laptop. "Last chance," she said. "Are you *sure* Glen?"

I looked mournfully at the screen, shaking my head uselessly.

Absolutely, said Lance. *Knock him dead!*

I saw her minimize the chat window and leave the room. Moments later, she was back...with Tony. He was wearing a short-sleeve shirt that emphasized his powerful forearms, and his hair was wet, as if he'd just taken a shower. I wondered if he'd prepared for this just as much as she had.

I got up and started pacing the room, watching as Tony closed the door and then leaned back against it. I could see that Heather was nervous and flighty, sucking in air through her nostrils as she turned to face him, one heel tapping on the floor.

"So," Tony said. "Last night you sent me away. Tonight you want me back, and you're all dressed up like you're going to give a goddamn seminar. What gives?"

Of course, he knew exactly what was going on. He was in on the whole thing, damn him. But Heather didn't know that. She thought she had to play the cheating wife...and I knew that Lance and Tony would enjoy that to the full.

"I...." Heather nervously laced and unlaced her fingers. "I'm sorry I sent you away last night. I got nervous. I've never done this before."

"'This?'" Tony asked. "You mean—cheated on Glen?"

Heather blushed. "Yes."

"But you're going to, aren't you?" He took a step towards her. "You're going to cheat on him. With me."

Heather looked at the floor. "I—"

He waited. I got the impression that he wanted to hear her say it.

"Yes," she said in a small voice.

Something inside me died. Up until that moment, I'd hoped—prayed—that some inner morality would kick in, that she'd come to her senses and change her mind. Now, there was no hope.

"Come here," he told her.

She walked over to him, taking tiny steps. I saw her nervously lick her lips. When she reached him, he put a hand under her chin and tilted her head back.

"You're not going to change your mind again, are you, Heather?" he asked her, in the tone of a schoolteacher.

She shook her head dumbly.

His lips came down on hers and I heard her groan as his tongue slipped into her mouth. His hand traced down her cheek...then her shoulder...then her arm. When it moved across to her breast and squeezed her lightly, she didn't pull away.

Tony broke the kiss and turned her head to the side a little, facing away from the camera, so that he could kiss down her neck. And then, while she couldn't see, he turned to look straight at the laptop and grinned at me.

I wanted to hurl something through the screen. The bastard knew I was watching, and he was loving it!

He laid kisses down her throat and behind her ears and she started moaning softly in a way that made my stomach churn...and my cock swell. Despite everything, the sight of her being touched by another man still turned me on.

His hands were all over her breasts now, groping her...*mauling* her. She groaned at the rough treatment, but she didn't resist. If anything, she pressed her body closer to him.

A chat window popped up on the laptop—a new one.

I think she likes it a bit rough, Lance typed. He was talking directly to me, I realized. The keyboard was still locked out, but he could hear me and see me—my camera and mic were only blocked to Heather. *So he can enjoy my humiliation,* I fumed.

"Please," I begged. "Stop this."

But they're having so much fun, Lance typed. *Especially Heather. Doesn't it look like she's having fun, Glen?*

Tony's hands were on her ass now, pulling her hard against him, squeezing and kneading her firm cheeks while his mouth devoured her. As I watched, he dragged the skirt up a little—enough to reveal the tops of her hold-ups.

"Stockings" he said, pushing her back a little so he could see. "Did you wear those especially for me?"

Heather nodded, and he grinned.

I knew he'd like them, Lance typed to me. *See how helpful I am, Glen? Helping your wife get what she wants.*

"You bastard!" I shouted at the laptop.

Lance didn't answer. Probably too busy laughing.

Tony's hands grew frantic. He unbuttoned her blouse, popping the buttons so quickly I thought he was going to tear them off. Then he skimmed his hands under her blouse, around her back, and unfastened her bra. He pushed it up out of the way, and we were all gazing at my wife's beautiful breasts.

She's really hot, Lance commented to me. *Seriously, Glen. Thank you for allowing her on board. I mean, most men would have had more sense than to send their wife to an oil rig for weeks, all on her own. You're really generous. Or really stupid.*

I stared at the screen, my eyes hot.

Oh, are you going to cry for us? Lance asked. *Poor little Glen. About to see his wife get fucked.*

I slammed the laptop shut and it went into sleep mode, Heather's moans cutting off suddenly. I paced the lounge, my hands in my hair.

I couldn't watch.

I couldn't *not* watch.

I opened up the laptop again, in time to see

Tony push Heather onto the bed. She was panting, and landed with her legs slightly apart. Her skirt was up around her hips, her naked breasts bouncing as she stared up at him.

He climbed onto the bed, undoing his belt.

"No," I said aloud, shaking my head. "No. I don't want this. Do you understand? I don't want this!"

Your cock says you do, typed Lance.

I looked down. My cock was rock hard against my thigh, the bulge in my pants obvious. I'd forgotten that Lance could still see my camera feed. He knew the truth about how this was affecting me...maybe better than I did.

Tony had his jeans down now and was pushing down his jockey shorts. Heather gasped as she saw his cock and then, as he turned slightly, I gasped, too. He was big—at least half as big as me again, and thick. The head of his cock was plum-like, heavy and swollen.

Oh dear, Glen, typed Lance. *Look at that. Bigger than yours, isn't it?*

I said nothing, merely stared.

Tony fisted his cock and held it for Heather to see. "Do you want this?" he asked her.

She swallowed nervously, but nodded.

"You look scared," he said. "Is it bigger than Glen's?"

He knew, of course. He'd watched the video of me jacking off—I was sure of it. This was just to humiliate me.

Heather gave a tiny glance at the camera. She

knew I was watching. But she also thought I was enjoying the whole thing. "Y—Yes," she said.

"I bet you always told your husband his was normal, didn't you?" asked Tony. "You're that sort of girl. Considerate."

She didn't answer, so he kissed her neck and nibbled her earlobe. "Didn't you?" he pressed.

"Yes...." she said softly.

LOL, typed Lance.

I glared at the letters. Not only was Heather being shown a bigger, better cock than mine, not only was Tony about to fuck her, but I was well aware that Lance would be recording this whole thing. Tomorrow, all the other guys on the rig would watch it and laugh at Heather's small-cocked husband. The worst part was that she'd lied to me— with good intentions, true, but still a lie. I'd always thought I was average. Now I knew I was small.

Tony reached up under her skirt and dragged her thong down her legs and off, tossing it aside. He pushed her skirt up a little more, so that she was completely exposed. Thanks to her shaved pussy, I could see her soft, pink lips, already swollen with arousal. There was a glint of moisture between them.

She's wet for him, Lance typed. *Your darling wife is wet for another guy, Glen.*

"Shut up!" I roared, thumping my fist on the table.

Tony lowered himself between my wife's legs. I saw her glance at the laptop screen for a second, checking to see if "RED" had appeared in the taskbar. But of course it hadn't—because Lance hadn't typed it. And he never would.

Suddenly, Heather gasped, her gaze snapping back to Tony. He wasn't in her yet, but I could see him making small movements.

"Does that feel good, Heather?" he asked.

"Yesss," Heather breathed.

I realized he was rubbing up and down her pussy lips with the head of his erect cock.

I froze. His *naked* cock. He hadn't put a condom on.

"Wait!" I yelled. "Wait! Stop him!"

I saw Tony put his hands on Heather's thighs and push her legs apart as far as the narrow bed allowed.

"Stop!" I shouted. "He's not using a condom!"

I'm sure he's clean, Lance typed.

"Here it comes," Tony told Heather, shifting closer to her. I heard her gasp, saw her eyes open wide as she felt the head of his cock pressing at her now spread entrance.

"You don't understand! She's not on the pill!" I was clutching at the table, my knuckles white. "Stop him! Stop him!"

Oh dear, Lance typed. *So poor Heather could get knocked up?*

Tony pushed forward and groaned. I couldn't see his cock entering her, but I didn't need to—everything I needed was written on Heather's beautiful face. I saw her lips part as he stretched her wide, her head come off the pillow...and then the sudden gasp as the head of his cock slid inside her.

"Stop him!" I shouted. "Lance, stop him!"

Hmm, typed Lance, as if debating. *Well, what a dilemma.*

Tony sank a little further down and I imagined that big, hard cock spreading her delicate tunnel wider. The swollen head of him plunging deeper, deeper. His balls, loaded with sperm—he could come at any second!

"Please!" I was beside myself, now. If Heather returned having slept with another guy, we could come back from that...maybe. But if she got pregnant by someone else.... "We're trying for a baby!"

Well then, typed Lance, *we're giving you what you want.*

Available for your Kindle, Nook, cell phone or PC at any of these retailers: Amazon, Barnes & Noble, Google Play and All Romance Ebooks.

Victoria Kasari

OTHER BOOKS BY VICTORIA KASARI

Cuckolded - Watching My Wife

I only wanted to save my marriage. When my wife told me she fantasized about sex with another man, I thought it'd be the perfect way to get our sex life back. I thought I'd be the one in control.... I made the mistake of introducing my wife to Greg: moneyed, handsome and black. I didn't know that Greg had a cruel streak a mile wide...that he'd turn my innocent wife into his whore, and force me to watch him take her, unable to stop them: not once, but time and time again. I didn't know that he had plans to use her body in every way he could, or to breed her...I didn't know that I'd be cuckolded, or how humiliating it would be. This is my story.

Cuckolded 2 - My Best Friend's Wife

Mark thought his life couldn't get any worse. He's already seen his beautiful wife taken and bred by black, alpha male Greg. Now Greg's back, and has his eye on Megan, the wife of Mark's best friend. Mark is faced with an impossible choice: help Greg cuckold his best friend and see innocent redhead Megan suffer the same fate as his wife Carla, or Greg will lead Carla even deeper into degradation.

But Greg's not to be trusted... and with two women at his beck and call and two men to cuckold, the possibilities are even greater...

Cuckolded in College

I'm a geek. I admit it. When I somehow landed a girlfriend like Olivia - a beautiful, smart redhead - I thought all my problems were over.

They were just beginning.

She needed more than I could give her in bed. When she met Leroy, the black, muscled football captain, she claimed to hate him... but seemed to be drawn to him like a moth to the flame. I had to watch her make what I knew was a dangerous bet with him. And when it all went wrong, I had to watch my girlfriend fucked - and bred - again and again. We were in much too deep - and there was nothing I could do to stop it.

Cuckolded By My Boss (Four Part Series)

My wife and I work for the same company. Our problems started when the new, black CEO made me redundant. I came up with a plan to get my revenge and set my wife and I up for life. I convinced her to lead him on, and I planned to film him kissing her and sue his ass for sexual harassment.

It all went horribly wrong. Things went too far, and my boss found out about my plan. Suddenly, the tables were turned—now my boss was determined to fuck my wife and make me watch. Not just once, but again and again, in one degrading, humiliating situation after another. I never guessed that my beautiful, shy wife longed to be treated like a slut, or that once she'd had a taste of my black boss's cock, I'd never be enough for her again....

Cuckolded - My Wife on the Oil Rig

Three weeks on an oil rig, and she'd be the only woman on board. I wasn't worried at all: my wife was completely faithful. In fact, I even encouraged her to tease the oil workers while I watched via webcam.

Then things went horribly wrong. The head of the rig hacked my laptop and, pretending to be me, encouraged my wife to go further and further with him and his buddies. Thousands of miles away, all I could do was watch in horror as they took her again and again....

Cuckolded - My Wife at the Renaissance Faire

My wife dressed up as a buxom wench, plenty of mead...what could be better? I even encouraged her to flirt with some of the guys while I watched. It was just innocent fun.

But then she attracted the attention of the king, and with the help of his friends and a jester costume, he convinced her that I was happy for her to go further and further. Bound and gagged, I could only watch in horror as she lived out her secret, submissive fantasies and let all of them take her again and again....

The Cuckolded in Revenge Trilogy

An epic series (116,000 words in total) that sees a man first falsely imprisoned and cuckolded, then feminized and eventually sissified. All three parts are now available, so you won't be left hanging.

1 - Locked Up and Cuckolded

When I discovered someone at my company was laundering money, I went to the authorities. I didn't know my boss was behind the whole thing...or that he'd frame me and send me to jail. But that was only the start of his revenge. He seduced my lonely wife, taking her again and again. Worse, he filmed all of it and made me watch it, helpless in my jail cell....

2 - Feminized and Cuckolded

I'd been framed and sent to jail by Kyle Dacosta, forced to watch from my cell as he took my wife again and again. Now, he'd agreed with the corrupt local authorities that he could "rehabilitate" me in his mansion. I'd have to live under the same roof as my worst enemy, made to watch as he took my wife, shared her with others and did his best to get her pregnant. But that wasn't enough for him. He wanted to transform me into a sexy, obedient woman and train me to service him and his male friends. I was about to be feminized....

3 - Sissified and Cuckolded

I'd been imprisoned, feminized and forced to live with the man who was cuckolding me. But if I thought my humiliation was complete, I'd underestimated Kyle's cruelty. He wanted to complete my transformation into a sissy by having me service his male party guests. Meanwhile, he lent my wife to his buddy Russ...and I was made to watch as he, too, seduced her. Kyle thought he'd broken me completely. Was he right? Or was I finally about to turn the tables?